MESSENGER'S
LEGACY

MESSENGER'S LEGACY

Peter V. Brett

HARPER
Voyager

HarperCollins*Publishers*
77–85 Fulham Palace Road,
Hammersmith, London W6 8JB

www.harpervoyagerbooks.co.uk

Published by Harper*Voyager*
An imprint of HarperCollins*Publishers* 2014
1

Peter V. Brett asserts the moral right to
be identified as the author of this work

A catalogue record for this book
is available from the British Library

ISBN: 978-0-00-811470-1

This novel is entirely a work of fiction.
The names, characters and incidents portrayed in it are
the work of the author's imagination. Any resemblance to
actual persons, living or dead, events or localities is
entirely coincidental.

Set in Sabon LT Std by Palimpsest Book Production Limited,
Falkirk, Stirlingshire

Printed and bound in Great Britain by
Clays Ltd, St Ives plc

MIX

Find out

For Myke and Joshua, who read all the versions.

Introduction

Like the other Demon Cycle novellas, *The Great Bazaar* and *Brayan's Gold*, this story grew out of the main series, a stunted branch that put down roots and flourished when planted on its own.

The first chapter, 'Burning True', was originally written as the opening chapter of my third novel, *The Daylight War*. It quickly became clear that telling Briar's story fully would require far more space than I had to spare in a series already known for its ever-increasing number of point-of-view characters. The chapter was excised, but I always knew I would come back to it when the time was right.

Some time later, the chapter was published in Shawn Speakman's charity anthology *Unfettered*, under the title *Mudboy*. Still only a piece of Briar's story, I'm grateful to Subterranean Press for giving me the chance now to finally tell the story in full.

Look for Briar to make appearances in *The Skull Throne*, the fourth book of the Demon Cycle next year.

Peter V. Brett
July, 2014
www.petervbrett.com

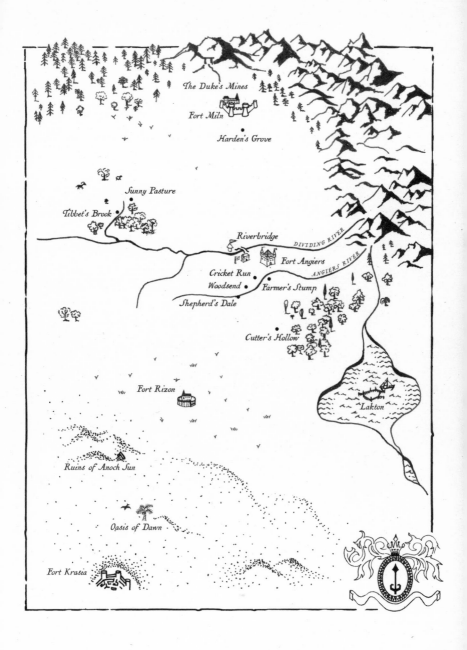

1

Burning True
324 AR Summer

Briar started awake at the clanging.

His mother was banging the porridge pot with her metal ladle, the sound echoing through the house. 'Out of bed, lazeabouts!' she cried. 'First Horn sounded a quarter past and breakfast is hot! Any who ent finished by sunup get an empty belly till luncheon!'

A pillow struck Briar's head. 'Open the slats, Briarpatch,' Hardey mumbled.

'Why do I always have to do it?' Briar asked.

Another pillow hit Briar on the opposite side of his head. 'Cause if there's a demon there, Hardey and I can run while it eats you!' Hale snapped. 'Get goin'!'

The twins always bullied him together . . . not that it mattered. They had twelve summers, and each of them towered over him like a wood demon.

Briar stumbled out of the bed, rubbing his eyes as he felt his way to the window and turned up the slats. The sky was a reddish purple, giving just enough light for Briar to make out the lurking shapes of demons in the yard. His mother called them cories, but Father called them *alagai*.

While the twins were still stretching in bed waiting for their eyes to adjust to the light, Briar hurried out of the room to try and be first to the privy curtain. He almost made it, but as usual, his sisters shouldered him out of the way at the last second.

'Girls first, Briarpatch!' Sky said. With thirteen summers, she was more menacing than the twins, but even Sunny, ten, could muscle poor Briar about easily.

He decided he could hold his water until after breakfast, and made it first to the table. It was Sixthday. The day Relan had bacon, and each of the children was allowed a slice. Briar inhaled the smell as he listened to the bacon crackle on the skillet. His mother was folding eggs, singing to herself. Dawn was a round woman, with big meaty arms that could wrestle five children at once, or crush them all in an embrace. Her hair was bound in a green kerchief.

Dawn looked up at Briar and smiled. 'Bit of a chill lingering in the common, Briar. Be a good boy and lay a fire to chase it off, please.'

Briar nodded, heading into the common room of their small cottage and kneeling at the hearth. He reached up the chimney, hand searching for the notched metal bar of the flue. He set it in the open position, and began laying the fire. From the kitchen, he heard his mother singing.

When laying the fire, what do you do?
Open the flue, open the flue!
Then leaves and grass blades and kindle sticks strew
Pile bricks of peat moss, two by two
Bellow the embers till the heat comes through
And watch the fire, burning true.

Briar soon had the fire going, but his brothers and sisters made it to the table by the time he returned, and they gave him no room to sit as they scooped eggs and fried tomatoes with onions onto their plates. A basket of biscuits sat steaming on the table as Dawn cut the rasher of bacon. The smells made Briar's stomach howl. He tried to reach in to snatch a biscuit, only to have Sunny slap his hand away.

'Wait your turn, Briarpatch!'

'You have to be bold,' said a voice behind him, and Briar turned to see his father. 'When I was in Sharaj, the boy who was too timid went hungry.'

His father, Relan asu Relan am'Damaj am'Kaji, had been a *Sharum* warrior once, but had snuck from the Desert Spear in the back of a Messenger's cart. Now he worked as a refuse collector, but his spear and shield still hung on the wall. His children all took after him, dark-skinned and whip thin.

'They're all bigger than me,' Briar said.

Relan nodded. 'Yes, but size and strength are not everything, my son.' He glanced to the front door. 'The sun will rise soon. Come watch with me.'

Briar hesitated. His father's attention always seemed to be on his older brothers, and it was wonderful to be noticed, but he remembered the demons he had seen in the yard. A shout from his mother turned both their heads.

'Don't you dare take him out there, Relan! He's only six! Briar, come back to the table.'

Briar moved to comply, but his father put a hand on his shoulder, holding him in place. 'Six is old enough to be caught by *alagai* for running when it is best to keep still, beloved,' Relan said, 'or for keeping still when it is best to run. We do our children no favours by coddling them.' He guided Briar onto the porch, closing the door before Dawn could retort.

The sky was a lighter shade of indigo now, dawn only minutes away. Relan lit his pipe, filling the porch with its sweet, familiar scent. Briar inhaled deeply, feeling safer with his father's smoke around him than he did with the wards.

Briar looked about in wonder. The porch was a familiar place, filled like the rest of their home with mismatched furniture Relan had salvaged from the town dump and carefully mended.

But in the false light before dawn everything looked different – bleak and ominous. Most of the demons had fled the coming sun by now, but one had turned at the creak of the porch door and the light and sound that came from the house. It caught sight of Briar and his father, stalking towards them.

'Keep behind the paint,' Relan warned, pointing with his pipe stem to the line of wards on the planks. 'Even the boldest warrior does not step across the wards lightly.'

The wood demon hissed at them. Briar knew it – the one that rose each night by the old goldwood tree he loved to climb. The demon's eyes were fixed on Relan, who met its gaze coolly. The demon charged, striking the wardnet with its great branchlike arms. Silver magic spiderwebbed through the air. Briar shrieked and ran for the house.

His father caught his wrist, yanking him painfully to a stop. 'Running attracts their attention.' He pulled Briar around to see that, indeed, the demon's gaze was turned his way. A thin trickle of drool, yellow like sap, ran from the corner of its mouth as it gave a low growl.

Relan squatted and took Briar by the shoulders, looking him in the eyes. 'You must always respect the *alagai*, my son, but you should never be ruled by your fear of them.'

He gently pushed the boy back towards the wards. The demon was still there, stalking not ten feet away. It shrieked at him, maw opening to reveal rows of amber teeth and a rough brown tongue.

Briar's leg began to twitch, and he ground his foot down to try and still it. His bladder felt about to burst. He bit his lip. His brothers and sisters would never tire of teasing if he went back inside with a wet pant leg.

'Breathe, my son,' Relan said. 'Embrace your fear and trust in the wards. Learn their ways, and inevera, you will not die on *alagai* talons.'

Briar knew he should trust his father, who had stood out in the night with nothing but his shield and spear, but the words did nothing to stop the churning in his stomach, or the need to pee. He crossed his legs to help hold back his water, hoping his father wouldn't notice. He looked at the horizon, but it was still orange, with no hint of yellow.

Already, he could see his brothers rolling on the floor with laughter as his sisters sang, 'Pissy pants! Pissy pants! Water in the Briarpatch!'

'Look to me, and I will teach you a Baiter's trick,' Relan said, allowing the boy to step back. His father toed the wards instead, looking the wood demon in the eye and returning its growl.

Relan leaned to the left, and the demon mimicked him. He straightened and leaned to the right, and the wood demon did the same. He began to sway slowly from side to side, and like a reflection in the water, the demon followed, even as Relan took a step to the left, then went back to his original position, then took a step to the right. The next time he took two steps in either direction. Then three. Each time, the demon followed.

His father took four exaggerated steps to the left, then stopped, leaning his body back to the right. Instinctively, the demon began stepping to the right, following the pattern, even as Relan broke it, resuming his steps to the left. He reached the far side of the porch before the demon caught on, letting out a shriek and leaping for him. Again the wards flared, and it was cast back.

Relan turned back to Briar, dropping to one knee to meet the boy's eyes.

'The *alagai* are bigger than you, my son. Stronger, too. But', he flicked Briar's forehead with his finger, 'they are not smarter. The servants of Nie have brains as tiny as a shelled pea, slow to think and easy to dazzle. If you are caught out with one, embrace your fear and sway as I have taught you. When the *alagai* steps the wrong way, walk – do not run – towards the nearest succour. The smartest demon will take at least six steps before growing wise to the trick.'

'*Then* you run,' Briar guessed.

Relan smiled, shaking his head. 'Then you keep walking the span of three slow breaths. It will be that long at least before the demon reorientates.' He smacked Briar's thigh, making him wince and clutch at his crotch, trying to hold the water in. '*Then* you run. Run as if the house were on fire.'

Briar nodded, grimacing.

'Three breaths,' Relan said again. 'Take them now.' He sucked in a breath, inviting Briar to follow. He did, filling his lungs, then breathing out with his father. Again Relan drew, and Briar followed.

He knew it was meant to calm him, but the deep breathing only seemed to make the pressure worse. He was sure his father must be able to see it, but Relan gave no sign. 'Do you know why your mother and I named you Briar?'

Briar shook his head, feeling his face heat with the strain.

'There was once a boy in Krasia who was abandoned by his parents for being weak and sickly,' Relan said. 'He could not keep up with the herds they followed to survive, and his father, who already had many sons, cast him out.'

Tears began to stream down Briar's cheeks. Would his father cast him out as well, if he wet himself in fear?

'A pack of nightwolves that had been following the herd were frightened of the family's spears, but when they caught the boy's scent, alone and unprotected, they began to stalk him,' Relan continued. 'But the boy led them into a briar patch, and when one of the wolves followed him in, it became stuck in the sharp thorns. The boy waited until it was caught fast, then dashed its head in with a stone. When he returned to his father with the wolf's pelt around his shoulders, his father fell on his knees and begged Everam's forgiveness for doubting his son.'

Relan squeezed Briar's shoulders again. 'Your brothers and sisters may tease you for your name, but wear it proudly. Briar patches thrive in places no other plants can survive, and even the *alagai* respect their thorns.'

The need to empty his water did not go away, but Briar felt the urgency fade, and he straightened, standing with his father as they watched the sky fill with colour. The remaining demon faded into mist, sinking into the ground before the first sliver of the sun crested the horizon. Relan put his arm around Briar as they watched sunrise shimmer across the surface of the lake. Briar leaned in, enjoying the rare moment alone with his father, without the shoving and teasing of his siblings.

I wish I didn't have any brothers and sisters, he thought.

Just then, the sunlight struck him.

The others were stacking their dishes, but Dawn had left plates for Briar and Relan. Briar sat alone with his father, and felt very special.

Relan bit into his first strip of bacon and closed his eyes, savouring every chew. 'The *dama* used to tell me pig-eaters burned in Nie's abyss, but by the Creator's beard, I swear it a fair price.'

Briar mimicked him, biting into his slice and closing his eyes to savour the grease and salt.

'How come Briarpatch gets to eat after sunup?' Sky demanded.

'Yeah!' the twins echoed at once. If there was one thing they agreed with Sky about, it was bullying Briar.

The smile fell from Relan's face. 'Because he eats with me.' His tone made it clear further questions would be answered with his strap. The old strip of leather hung on the wall by the mantle, a warning all the Damaj children took very seriously. Relan used the strap to whip his mule when it refused a heavy load, but he had not hesitated to take it to Hardey's backside the time he threw a cat in the lake to see if it could swim. They all remembered their brother's howls, and lived in terror of that strap.

Relan paid his other children no further mind, taking a second slice of bacon on his fork and laying it on Briar's plate.

'Boys, feed the animals and get the dump cart hitched,' Dawn said, breaking the tension. 'Girls, get the laundry soaking.' The children bowed and quickly filed out, leaving Briar alone with his father.

'When a boy first stands before the *alagai* in Krasia, he is sent to spend the following day in prayer,' Relan said. He laughed. 'Though I admit, when I tried it, I soon grew bored. Still, it is wise to think on the experience. After prayers, you may take the rest of the day to walk in the sun.'

A day to do whatever he wished. Briar knew what to say, though the words seemed insufficient. 'Yes, Father. Thank you, Father.'

The Damaj family walked single file to the Holy House. Relan was in the lead, followed by Dawn. Hale came next, a quarter-hour older than Hardey. Sky was a year older than them both, but she was a girl and came after, followed by Sunny. When Briar was nine, he would move ahead of his sisters, but that was years away. He always came last, hurrying to keep up with the brutal pace Relan set.

They walked double-time today because of their late start. Briar could see in his siblings' eyes that they would make him pay for that, and for being excused from chores.

Even with the delay, the Damajes passed through Town Square as many folk were first opening their shutters to greet the morning. The Holy House was nearly empty.

'Disgusting,' Relan said, taking in the empty pews. A handful of Boggers, mostly elders, had come to pray, but it was only a fraction of those that came on Seventhday, and even that was not everyone in Bogton.

Briar knew his father's words before they were said. Relan was apt to rant on this topic for his children's benefit.

'It is an insult to Everam, that His children pray but once a week.' Normally, when Relan invoked insult to the Creator, he was apt to spit, but never in the Holy House. 'In Krasia, the *dama* would have the other townsfolk given a taste of the *alagai* tail. The next dawn, the temple would be full again.'

Aric Bogger, one of the greybeards from Town Square, turned and glared angrily at them. 'We disgust you so much, mudskin, why don't you go back to the desert?'

Relan grimaced, shoulders bunching. He claimed to have been no great warrior in Krasia, but in Bogton he was feared by all, and known to beat men for using that word. No one had dared insult his heritage since Masen Bales and his three brothers had called him a desert rat on Winter Solstice. Relan wasn't even breathing hard by the time all men were on the ground, moaning in submission.

But they were in the Holy House, and the man was an elder. Honour dictated that Relan show Aric deference and respect.

Relan closed his eyes, embracing his anger. His shoulders relaxed. He gave a shallow bow. 'You do not disgust me, Aric Bogger. You are humble before Everam. I see you here honouring Him every dawn.'

The words were meant to calm the situation, but they seemed to have the opposite effect as Aric thrust his cane down with a thump, surging to his feet.

'I am humble before the *Creator*, Relan Damaj.' Aric shifted his grip on his cane, raising it between them. 'I spit on your Everam.'

He hawked his throat, and Relan had enough. He closed the distance between them in an instant, his left hand effortlessly twisting the cane from Aric's grasp as his right darted in like a hummingbird to flick across the greybeard's throat.

Aric coughed as the phlegm caught in his throat, stumbling back a step before he caught himself on the pews. He didn't seem hurt, but his face went all red as he hacked and wheezed.

'I wish no quarrel with you, Aric son of Aric of the Bogger

clan of Bogton,' Relan said, 'but I will not stand by and let you spit on the floor of the Creator's house.'

Aric looked as if he might lunge at him, but Relan pointed the cane, checking the move.

'What's going on here?!' Briar turned to see Tender Heath gripping the front of his brown robes as he strode to the scene. Heath was not a threatening man, round-faced and round-bellied. He brewed the town ale, and was more apt to laugh than to scold, tending bar as much as he tended his flock.

But they saw Holy Men differently in Krasia. Relan stiffened, then dipped into a low bow. He gave a hiss, and his family joined him in bowing to the Tender. So much as a wilful eye would get them the strap and worse.

Relan twirled the cane, offering it handle-first for Aric to snatch. The old man looked as if he might strike Relan on his exposed neck, but a stern glance from the Tender checked him.

'A misunderstanding only, Tender,' Relan said. 'I was explaining to the son of Aric that we pray to the same Creator, whether He is called Everam or not.'

Heath crossed his meaty arms. 'That may be, but the Holy House is a place of peace and succour, Relan. We do not explain things at the end of a cane.'

Relan dropped smoothly to his knees, putting his hands and forehead on the floor in supplication. 'Of course the Tender is correct. I apologize and will accept penance.'

'Ay, give it to him, Tender,' Aric said, as the others in the room watched the scene. 'Stinking mudskin hit me.'

Heath looked at him. 'Don't think I don't know it was your fool mouth that started it, Aric Bogger. I catch you using the M word or try to spit in the Holy House again, you and yours are going to have empty cups at the next Solstice festival.'

Aric paled. The only thing Boggers loved more than the Creator was Heath's ale.

Tender Heath gave a sweep of his arm. 'Now into the pews,

the lot of you. Time we started services, and I'm feeling quite a sermon coming.'

'Mistress Dawn!' a call came, breaking the silence as they filed from the Holy House. Briar looked up to see Tami Bales running up the road. Tami was only a year older than Briar, but the Damaj children weren't allowed to play with the Baleses since Tami's father, Masen, called Relan a desert rat at the Solstice festival. Relan would have broken his arm if the other men hadn't pulled them apart.

Tami's dress was splattered with mud and red with blood. Briar knew bloodstains when he saw them. Any Animal Gatherer's child did. Dawn ran out to meet the girl, and Tami collapsed in her arms, panting for breath. 'Mistress . . . y-you have to save . . .'

'Who?' Dawn demanded. 'Who's been hurt? Corespawn it, girl, what's happened?'

'Corelings,' Tami gasped.

'Creator.' Dawn drew a ward in the air. 'Whose blood is this?' She pulled at the still-damp fabric of the girl's dress.

'Maybell,' Tami said.

Dawn's nose wrinkled. 'The cow?'

Tami nodded. 'Stuck her head over the pen, blocking one of the wardposts. Field demon clawed her neck. Pa says she's gonna get demon fever and went for his axe. Please, you need to come or he'll put her down.'

Dawn blew out a breath, shaking her head and chuckling. Tami looked ready to cry.

'I'm sorry, girl,' Dawn said. 'Don't mean to belittle. I know stock feels like part of the family sometimes. You just had me thinking it was one of your brothers or sisters got cored. I'll do what I can. Run and tell your pa to hold his stroke.'

She looked to Relan and the others. 'Girls, get home and

finish the washing. Boys, help your father haul the collection cart. Briar, I'll need to brew a sleep draught . . .'

'Skyflower and tampweed,' Briar nodded.

'Cut generously,' Dawn said. 'Takes a lot more to put down a cow than a person. We'll need hogroot poultices as well.'

Briar nodded. 'I know what to get.'

'Meet me in Masen Bales' yard,' Dawn said. 'Quick as you can.'

Briar ran off home, darting through the herb garden like a jackrabbit, then blowing through the kitchen like a breeze, snatching Dawn's mortar and pestle. He was on his way down the road before his siblings even got home.

He caught up with Dawn just as she was getting to the Bales farm with Tami. Already, he could hear Maybell's bleats of pain.

Masen Bales came out to meet them. He was carrying an axe. His eyes narrowed at the sight of Briar, and he spat some of the tobacco he was chewing. 'Thanks for coming, Gatherer. Think you're wasting a trip, though. Animal ent gonna make it.'

He led the way to the barn. The heifer was lying on the straw floor of her pen, neck wrapped in heavy cloth soaked through with blood. Masen Bales ran his thumb along the edge of his axe. Tami and her siblings crowded around the cow protectively, though none were large enough to stop their father if he decided it was Maybell's time.

Dawn lifted the cloth to look at the animal's wounds – three deep grooves in Maybell's thick neck.

Masen spat again. 'Meant to put the animal down quick and sell her to the butcher, but the kids begged me to wait till you came.'

'It's good you did,' Dawn said. 'This ent too bad, if we can stave off the infection.' She turned to the crowd of children. 'I'll need more cloth for bandages, buckets of clean water and a boiling kettle.' The children looked at her blankly until she clapped her hands, making them all jump. 'Now!'

As the children ran off, Briar laid out his mother's tools and began crushing the herbs for the sleeping draught and poultices. Getting the animal to drink was difficult, but soon Maybell was fast asleep, and Dawn cleaned out the wounds and inserted a thin paste of crushed herbs before stitching them closed.

Tami stood next to Briar, horrified. Briar had seen his mother work before, but he knew how scary it must seem. He reached out, taking Tami's hand, and she looked at him, smiling bravely in thanks as she squeezed tightly.

Masen had been watching Dawn work as well, but he glanced at Tami and did a double take, pointing his axe at Briar. 'Ay, get your muddy hands off my daughter, you little rat!'

Briar snatched his hand away in an instant. His mother stood, moving calmly between them as she wiped the blood from her hands. 'Ent going to need that axe any more, Masen, so I'd appreciate you not pointing it at my boy.'

Masen looked at the weapon in surprise, as if he'd forgotten he was holding it. He grunted and dropped the head, leaning it against the fence. 'Wasn't going to do anything.'

Dawn pursed her lips. 'That'll be twenty shells.'

Masen gaped. 'Twenty shells?! For stitching a cow?'

'Ten for the stitching,' Dawn said, 'and ten for the sleep draught and hogroot poultices my rat son made.'

'I won't pay it,' Masen said. 'Neither you nor your mud-skinned husband can make me.'

'I don't need Relan for that,' Dawn said, smiling, 'though we both know he could make you. No, all I need is to tell Marta Speaker you won't pay, and Maybell will be grazing in my yard before tomorrow.'

Masen glared. 'You ent been right in the head since you married that desert rat, Dawn. Already cost all your human custom. Lucky to get animal work these days, but that won't last when folk hear you're charging twenty shells for it.'

Briar's nostrils flared. If Relan was there, he would break

Masen's nose for speaking to his mother so disrespectfully. But Relan wasn't there, so it was Briar's responsibility.

His eyes ran over Masen Bales as he recalled the *sharusahk* lessons he had watched Relan give his brothers. Masen had a weak knee, always complaining about it when the weather was damp. One well-placed kick there . . .

Without turning, Dawn made her voice a stern murmur only the children could hear. 'Don't think your mum don't know what you're thinking, Briarpatch. You mind your hands and mouth.'

Briar flushed, putting his hands in his pockets as Dawn crossed her arms and took a step towards Masen. 'That's Mistress Dawn to you, Masen Bales, and now it's twenty-five. Call one more name, I'll go see Marta right now.'

Masen began muttering curses, but he stomped off to the house, coming back with a worn leather bag. He counted the smooth lacquered shells into Dawn's hand. 'Fifteen . . . sixteen . . . seventeen. That's all I got right now, *Mistress*. You'll have the rest in a week. Honest word.'

'I'd better,' Dawn said. 'Come along, Briar.'

The two of them walked down the road until they came to the fork, one way leading to their home, the other to the rest of town.

'You were very brave today, Briar,' his mother said.

'Wasn't right, what he said,' Briar said.

She waved a hand. 'Wasn't talking about that fool-headed Masen Bales. Meant in the yard this morning.'

Briar shook his head. 'Wasn't brave. Almost peed my pants I was so scared.'

'But you didn't,' Dawn said. 'Didn't scream or run away, didn't faint. That's all brave is. When you're scared, but keep your wits about you. Relan says you held up better than your brothers.'

'Really?' Briar asked.

'Really.' Dawn narrowed her eyes. 'You stir trouble by tellin' 'em I told you that, though, and it'll be the strap.'

Briar swallowed. 'I won't tell anyone.'

Dawn laughed and put her arms around him, squeezing tightly. 'Know you won't, poppet. I'm so proud of you. You run off now. Enjoy the sun for a few hours, like your da promised. I'll see you at supper.' She smiled and pressed a handful of shells into his hand.

'In case you want to buy a meat pie and some sugar candy.'

Briar felt a thrill as he made his way into town, running his fingers over the smooth lacquer of the shells. He'd never had money of his own before, and had to suppress a whoop of glee.

He went to the butcher shop, where Mrs Butcher sold hot meat pies, and laid a shell on the counter.

Mrs Butcher looked at him suspiciously. 'Where'd you get that shell, Mudboy? You steal it?'

Briar shook his head. 'Mother gave it to me for helping her save Tami Bales' cow.'

Mrs Butcher grunted and took the shell, handing him a steaming pie in return.

He went next to the sugarmaker, who fixed a glare on Briar the moment he came into the shop. His look did not soften until Briar produced a pair of shells to pay for the candies he collected from the display, all wrapped in twisted corn husks. These he stuffed in his pockets, eating the meat pie as he walked back out of town. The sun was bright on his shoulders, and it felt warm and safe. The memory of the wood demon snarling at him seemed a distant thing.

He walked down to the lake and watched the fishing boats for a time. It was a clear day, and he could just make out Lakton in the distance, the great city floating far out on the lake. He followed the shoreline, skipping stones across the water.

He stopped short, spotting a pair of webbed tracks in the mud left by a bank demon. He imagined the frog-like creature leaping onto the shore and catching him with its long sticky tongue. The tracks made him shiver, and suddenly he had to pee desperately. He barely lowered his pants in time, thankful there was no one to see.

'Brave,' he muttered to himself, knowing the lie for what it was.

Late in the afternoon, Briar hid behind the house and pulled out one of the sugar candies. He unwrapped the treasure and chewed slowly, savouring every bite as his father did with bacon.

'Ay, Briarpatch!' a voice called. Briar looked up to see Hardey and Hale approaching.

'Where'd you get that candy?' Hale called, balling a fist.

'We get to haul trash all day, and he gets extra bacon and candy?' Hardey asked.

'Don't think that's right, do you?' Hale said.

Briar knew this game. All the boys in Bogton knew to step lightly when the twins started asking each other questions.

His mind ran through all the things he might say, but he knew none of them would make any difference. His brothers were going to knock him down and take the candy, promising worse if he told their parents.

He ran. Over the woodpiles, quick as a hare, and then cut through the laundry lines as his brothers charged after him. Sunny and Sky were collecting the clean wash in baskets, and he barely missed running into them.

'Ay, watch it, Briarpatch!' Sky shouted.

'Stop him, he's got candy!' he heard Hardey cry. Briar dodged around a hanging sheet and kept low as he doubled back around the house, running into the bog out back.

He could hear the others close behind, but the trees were thick before the ground became too damp, giving cover as he made for the goldwood tree where the wood demon rose. Briar had climbed the goldwood a hundred times and, knew every knot and branch. He swung up into its boughs like he was a wood demon himself, then froze and held his breath. The others ran by, and Briar counted fifty breaths before he dared move.

There was a small hollow where the branches met. Briar packed the candy in dry leaves and left it hidden there, praying to the Creator it would not rain. Then he dropped back to the ground and ran home.

At supper, his brothers and sisters watched him like a cat watches a mouse. Briar kept close to his mother until bedtime.

No sooner had the door to the tiny room the three boys shared closed, than the twins pinned him on the floor of their room, digging through his pockets and searching his bed.

'Where'd you hide them, Briarpatch?' Hardey demanded, sitting hard on his stomach, knocking the breath out of him.

'It was just the one, and I ate it!' Briar struggled, but he was wise enough not to raise his voice. A shout might get his brothers the strap, but it would go worse for him.

Eventually the boys gave up, giving him a last shake and going to bed. 'This ent over, Briarpatch,' Hardey said. 'Catch you with it later, you'll be eating dirt.'

They were soon asleep, but Briar's heart was still thumping, and out in the yard demons shrieked as they tested the wards. Briar couldn't sleep through the sound, flinching at every cry and flash of magic. Hale kicked him under the covers. 'Quit squirming, Briarpatch, or I'll lock you out on the porch for the night.'

Briar shuddered, and again felt an overwhelming urge to empty his bladder. He got out of bed and stumbled into the hall to find the privy. It was pitch black in the house, but that had never bothered Briar before. He had blindly fumbled his way to the curtain countless times.

But it was different tonight. There was a demon in the house.

Briar couldn't say how he knew, but he sensed it lurking in the darkness, waiting for its chance to pounce.

Briar could feel his heart pounding like a festival drum and began to sweat, though the night was cool. It was suddenly hard for him to breathe, as if Hardey were still sitting on his chest. There was a rustling sound ahead, and Briar yelped, literally jumping. He looked around and it seemed he could make out a dim shape moving in the darkness.

Terrified, he turned and ran for the common room. The fire had burned down, but a few pumps of the bellows had an open flame, and Briar fed it carefully with bricks of peat from the pile until it filled the room with light. Shadows fled, and with them the hiding places of the demons.

The room was empty.

Baby Briar, scared of nothing, his brothers and sisters liked to sing. Briar hated himself, but his leg would not stop shaking. He couldn't go back to bed. He would piss on the covers and the twins would kill him. He couldn't go down the hall to the privy in the dark. The very thought terrified him. He could sleep here, by the fire, or . . .

Briar slipped across the common to the door of his parents' room.

Never open the door if the bed is creaking, his mother had said, but Briar listened closely, and the bed was quiet. He turned the latch and slipped quietly inside, closing the door behind him. He crawled up the centre of the bed, nestling himself between his parents. His mother put her arms about him, and Briar fell deep asleep.

It was still dark when he awoke to screaming. His parents started upright, taking poor Briar with them. All of them took a reflexive breath, and started to cough and choke.

There was smoke everywhere. His parents were both touching

him, but he couldn't see them at all. Everything was a grey blur even worse than darkness.

'Down!' his mother croaked, pulling Briar with her as she slid off the bed. 'Smoke rises! The air will be better by the floor-boards.' There was a thump as his father rolled out of bed on the far side, crawling over to them.

'Take Briar out the window,' Relan said, coughing into his hand. 'I'll get the others and follow.'

'Into the night?!' Dawn asked.

'We cannot stay here, beloved,' Relan said. 'The wardposts in the herb garden are strong. It's only twenty yards from the house. You can make it if you are quick.'

Dawn grabbed Briar's hand, squeezing so hard the boy whimpered. 'Wet the towel by the washbasin and put it over your mouth to hold out the smoke.'

Relan nodded and put a hand on her shoulder. 'Be careful. The smoke will draw many *alagai*.' He kissed her. 'Go.'

Dawn began crawling for the window, dragging Briar after her. 'Take three deep breaths, Briar, and then hold the last. Keep it held until we're out the window, and as soon as we hit the ground, run for the garden. You understand?'

'Yes,' Briar said, and then coughed for what seemed forever. At last the wracking ceased, and he nodded to his mother. On the third breath, they stood and Dawn threw open the shutters. She lifted Briar in her arms, swung her legs over the sill, and dropped to the ground with a thump.

As Relan had warned, there were demons in the yard, flitting about through the drifting smoke. Together, they ran for the garden before the corelings caught sight of them.

Dawn stopped up short once they crossed the garden wards. 'You stay here. I need to help your father with the others.'

'No!' Briar cried, gripping her skirts. 'Don't leave me!'

Dawn gripped Briar's shirt tightly with one hand, and slapped his face with the other. His head seemed to flash with light, and he stumbled back, letting go her skirts.

'Ent got time to baby you right now, Briar. You mind me,' his mother said. 'Go to the hogroot patch and hide in the leaves. Cories hate hogroot. I'll be back soon.'

Briar sniffed and wiped at his tears, but he nodded and his mother turned and ran for the house. A wood demon caught sight of her and ran to intercept. Briar screamed.

But Dawn kept her head, doing the same dance Relan had done that very morning. In a moment, she had the coreling stumbling left as she ran to the right, disappearing back through the window.

Feeling numb, like he was in a dream, Briar stumbled over to the hogroot patch. He rolled in the thick weeds, bruising them and getting sticky hogroot sap all over himself. One of his pant legs was soaked through. He had pissed himself after all. The twins would never stop teasing him once they saw.

He cowered there, shaking, as his family's cries echoed in the night. He could hear them calling to one another, bits of sentences drifting on the night smoke to reach his ears. But no one came to the garden, and moments later, the night began to brighten, the grey smoke giving off an evil, pulsing glow. Briar looked up, and saw that the ghostly orange light came from the windows of the house.

The shrieks of the demons increased at the sight, and they clawed the dirt impatiently, waiting for the wards to fail. A wood demon struck at the house, and was thrown back by the magic. A flame demon tried to leap onto the porch, and it, too, was repelled. But even Briar could see that the magic was weakening, its light dimming.

When a wood demon tried the porch, the wardnet had weakened enough for it to power through. Magic danced over the demon's skin and it screamed in agony, but made it to the front door and kicked it in. A gout of fire, like a giant flame demon's spit, coughed out of the doorway, immolating the demon. It fell back, shrieking and smouldering, but a pack of flame demons had made it through the gap by then and disappeared into the house. Their gleeful shrieks filled the night, partially drowning out his family's dwindling screams.

Hardey stumbled out the side door, screaming. His face was dark with soot and splattered with gore, and one arm hung limply, the sleeve wet with blood. He looked about frantically.

Briar stood up. 'Hardey!' He jumped up and down, waving his arms.

'Briar!' Hardey saw him and ran for the garden wards, his usual long stride marred by a worsening limp. A pair of howling flame demons followed him out of the house, but Hardey had a wide lead as he raced for the hogroot patch.

But the boy hadn't cleared half the distance when a wind demon swooped down, digging its clawed feet deep into his back. Its wing talons flashed, and Hardey's head thumped to the ground. Before the body even began to fall, the wind demon snapped its wings and took to the air again, taking the rest of Hardey with it. Briar screamed as the demon vanished into the smoky darkness.

The flame demons shrieked at the departing wind demon for stealing their prey, but then leapt onto Hardey's head in a frenzy. Briar fell back into the hogroot patch, barely turning over in time to retch up his supper. He screamed and cried, thrashing about and trying to wake himself up from the nightmare, but on it went.

It grew hotter and hotter where Briar lay, and the smoke soon became unbearable. Burning ash drifted through the air like snowflakes, setting fires in the garden and yard. One flake struck Briar on the cheek and he shrieked in pain, slapping himself repeatedly in the face to knock the ash away.

Briar bit his lip to try and stem the wracking coughs, looking around frantically. 'Mother! Father! Anybody!' He wiped at the tears streaking the ash on his face. How could his mother leave him? He was only six!

Six is old enough to be caught by alagai *for running when it is best to keep still*, Relan said, *or for keeping still when it is best to run.*

He would burn up if he stayed any longer, but as his father said, the fire was drawing demons like moths. He thought of the goldwood tree. It had hidden him from his brothers and sisters. Perhaps it could succour him now.

Briar put his head close to the ground and breathed three times as his mother had told him, then sprang from hiding, running hard for the tree line. The swirling smoke was everywhere, and he could only see a few feet in any direction, but he could sense demons lurking in the gloom. He raced quickly over the familiar ground, but then somehow ran into a tree where he was sure none should be. He scraped his face on the bark, bouncing and landing on his back.

But then the tree looked at him and growled.

Briar slowly got to his feet, not making any sudden moves. The wood demon watched him curiously.

Briar began to sway back and forth like a pendulum, and the demon began rocking in unison, moving to keep eye contact like a tree swaying in a great wind. It began to step with him, and Briar held his breath as he moved two steps, then back, then three steps, then back, then, on the fourth step, he kept on walking. Three breaths later, the demon shook its head and Briar broke into a run.

The demon shrieked and gave chase. At first Briar had a fair lead, but the wood demon closed the gap in just a few great strides.

Briar dodged left and right, but the demon kept pace, its growls drawing ever nearer. He scrambled over the smouldering woodpile, but the demon scattered the logs with a single swipe of its talons. He skidded to a stop by his father's refuse cart, still loaded with some of the items Relan and his brothers had salvaged from the dump.

Briar dropped to his hands and knees, crawling under the

cart. He held his breath as the demon's clawed feet landed with a thump right in front of him.

The wood demon lowered its toothy snout to the ground, snuffling. It moved to the hollow, sniffing the roots and dirt. Briar knew the demon could reach under and fish him out, or toss the cart aside easily, but perhaps that would give him enough time to run out the other side and get to the tree. He waited as the snout drew closer, coming just a few inches from him.

Just then, the demon gave a tremendous sneeze, its rows of sharp amber teeth mere inches from Briar as the mouth opened and snapped shut.

Briar bolted from hiding, but the demon, gagging and coughing, did not immediately give chase.

The hogroot, Briar realized.

A small flame demon, no bigger than a coon, challenged him as he drew close to the tree, but this time Briar didn't try to run. He waited for the demon to draw close, then flapped his arms and clothes, creating a cloud of hogroot stink even in the acrid night. The demon heaved as if sick, and Briar kicked it, sending it sprawling as he ran on. He leapt to catch the first branch and swung himself up into the goldwood and hid in the boughs before the demon could recover.

Briar looked back and saw the windows of his house blazing like the hearth, flames licking out to climb their way up the walls.

The hearth.

Even from this distance, the heat could be felt, smoke and ash thick in the air, making every breath burn his lungs. But even so, Briar's face went cold. His leg twitched, and he felt it warm as his bladder let go what little it had left. In his mind, he could hear his mother singing.

> *When laying morning fire, what do you do?*
> *Open the flue, open the flue!*

How many times had he laid that fire? His father always closed off the chimney flue after the evening fire burned down. In the morning, you had to open it . . .

'Or the house will fill with smoke,' he whispered.

A minute ago, Briar had been feeling quite brave, but that was over. *Brave is when you're scared,* his mother said, *but keep your wits about you.*

Whatever Briar was, he wasn't that.

He dug in the hollow where the branches met, finding his hidden trove of sugar candies, and let them fall to the ground as he began to weep.

I should have just shared.

2

Briarpatch
324 AR Summer

It was not quite dawn, but light enough for Briar to see, when the cories started to fade away, like the smoke in the air. The flames had died out some time ago, leaving most of their house intact. Relan had never trusted wooden walls, and had built his home out of hundreds of stones salvaged from the town dump.

'Only fools', Relan said, 'throw away good stone to build with something weaker.'

The air grew quiet as the shrieks and howls of the demons faded away. Briar held his breath, listening, then slipped down from the goldwood tree.

'Never set foot outside the house till you can step in a sunbeam,' his mother had taught, but Briar could not wait another moment. He ran towards the house.

'Mother! Father! Sky! Sunny! Hale!' Briar was about to add Hardey to the call when he came upon the blackened remains of his brother's head. The demons had gnawed away the flesh and cracked the skull to scoop out the insides.

Briar steadied himself, wetting his shirt in the rain barrel and tying it over his face as he headed for the house. Smoke hung thick in the air, but already it was lessening. The thatched roof was gone, shutters were blown out and just a few broken boards hanging from a twisted iron hinge were all that remained of the front door.

His bare feet crunched on the warm ashes of reeds in the entryway. He froze for a moment, as if expecting a demon to leap at the sound, but shook the feeling away, continuing forwards. 'Mother? Father? Anyone?'

His foot squelched on the next step. Briar looked down, seeing blood everywhere. Some of it charred like drippings from a grill, other places wet and sticky. Bits of bone and gore were scattered through the common room where Briar had built up the fire.

Bloody demon footprints churned the greasy ash in every nook and corner of the small house. Briar was too horrified to even attempt to identify the remains, but it seemed there was enough to account for everyone, and to spare.

The stones Relan had carried and mortared stood strong, but the carefully mended furniture was a ruin, as was almost everything else. Briar salvaged a few scraps of clothing, but the food was all gone, and his mother's herbs and spices. All that remained was the big steel kitchen knife and her mortar and pestle. Briar took them.

He coughed, sending tendrils of pain through his chest. Even with his wet shirt over his face, the lingering smoke was too much.

He was about to leave when a glint of metal caught his eye in the common room. Amidst the bones and oily ash was his father's spear.

Briar reached to pull the weapon from the muck. The charred shaft broke off in his hand, but the head was still sharp and hard. Nearby he found Relan's warded shield. The straps would need mending, but the hammered bronze face still shone when he brushed the ash away.

Out on the porch he removed the shirt, breathing deep of the morning air just as sun struck railing. Was it just a day ago he had stood in this very spot with his father, clenching his legs and wishing he was an only child?

Everam heard my selfish wish, he thought. *He heard, and sent the cories to punish me by making it come true.*

Away in the distance he heard the Great Horn. Folk had seen the smoke and would be coming soon to investigate.

They won't know, he told himself. *Not that I started the fire, or that I made the wish.*

He sobbed. What did it matter if folk knew or not? He knew. Knew this was his fault. It was because of his selfishness. His stupidity. His carelessness.

I should have burned up with them, he thought. But that was wrong, too. His family had died with honour. They would walk the lonely path and sup at Everam's table in Heaven.

But there was no Heaven for Briar now. He was *khaffit.*

There were shouts from Boggers coming up the road. In a moment they would turn the corner and see him.

Briar turned and ran into the bog.

There was food enough in the bog, if you knew where to look. Birds built nests in the peat, and here and there were edible roots and herbs, obvious to a Gatherer's son. Briar wasn't very hungry anyway. A few mushrooms and roots to keep the stomach pains away, a sip of running water as he wandered. The bog went on as far as the eye could see, wetland all the way to the great lake fifty miles away.

Hours passed, and Briar found himself wandering to the dump along the outskirts of the bog. He'd been there countless times, riding on father's refuse cart.

Briar always found it peaceful. Few came here save his family, and Briar felt safe with the rest of the refuse, at least while the sun was high. The dump was a quiet graveyard, filled with the skeletons of carts and furniture that had passed beyond use, piled with mountains of smaller refuse, tall and stinking. Close to the bog, the ground was damp and soft, stinking even without the trash.

There was a wild hogroot patch behind one of the mountains of refuse, the weeds tall and thick, thriving in the composted soil.

Cories'll never find me there, Briar thought. The whole place stank too much for them to smell him, and demons wouldn't wander into a hogroot patch by accident.

Better'n sleeping in a briar patch.

3

Ragen
324 AR Summer

Ragen drew a deep breath. Some of it was his own stink after days on the road without a bed or bath, but greater was the scent of warm pollen to remind him why he loved the Messenger Road. It was summer in Lakton, something those in his home city of Miln, far to the north, could only read of and dream about. The rocky soil of the Milnese Mountains yielded reluctant fruit, but the fertile lands around the great lake gave without care.

He stood in his saddle, snatching an apple the size of his fist from a low-hanging branch. The villages along the road planted the trees with Messengers in mind. It was a point of pride with many villages, and those working the road could feast like kings on apple and pear, peach and plum. One stretch had oranges so fine just the memory could water Ragen's mouth.

Take your time, he thought, biting into the apple with a satisfying crunch. *Enjoy every moment and remember it, because you'll never see the like again.*

'A last tour,' he'd promised Elissa. 'I'll be back months before the babe comes, and hang up my spear for good.'

With the months on the road before him, it had been an easy promise to make. He made the most of the time, taking local mail runs to see old friends and say goodbyes. Some were cordial, others surprisingly moving. Correspondences were promised on both sides, but they all knew they would never see each other again.

He'd ridden all the way to Fort Rizon and beyond, travelling three more days just to visit a certain hill and look out over the desert flats one last time. But soon he would be leaving Lakton and entering Angiers, where his list of friends was thinner.

He longed to hold Elissa and see her swollen belly, but he could not help wishing for just a little more time before the gates of Miln closed on him for the final time.

Ragen had made this run every year for two decades, a trusted face welcomed by merchant and Royal alike. It was a coveted position senior Messengers would cut throats for – just a few years on that run would earn them enough for early retirement. Guildmaster Malcum was likely rubbing his hands with glee thinking of what Messengers would bid in return for the assignment.

But Ragen had already whispered in the right ears, and carried letters from Royals and merchants throughout the land asking for Ragen's ward, Arlen Bales, to take his place.

Ragen swallowed a lump of pride. Perhaps his tour was coming to a close, but it was fitting Arlen should take up where he left off, as Ragen had for his father, a Royal Messenger before him.

Ragen was jealous of Arlen, but it was his own future that weighed on him. Everyone spoke of his retirement as something desirable, like it should be some great relief to give up the beauty of the wide world and spend his remaining years on his backside behind warded walls.

'Night, I'm barely forty,' he muttered.

Forty-three, his inner voice answered. *Used to take four hours and a plate of eggs to shake off a night's drinking. Now your body aches for days.*

'You've got two choices as a Messenger,' Master Cob told him back when Ragen was his apprentice. 'Retire young, or die young. Demons aren't forgiving when you can't move as fast as you did when you were thirty.'

At last, the peat-farming village of Bogton came into sight on the road ahead, drawing Ragen's mind from his problems. Soon he would be with his friend Relan and his family, and could enjoy a warm meal and a laugh. Krasian goods were expensive in Fort Rizon, but nothing like the duke's ransom they were in Miln. His saddlebags bulged with Krasian toys for the children, silk and spices for Dawn, and an entire jug of couzi for Relan.

Ragen smiled. For Relan, perhaps, but for himself as well. One last time, they would drink till they tasted cinnamon and spend the night terrifying Dawn and the children with tales of their adventures on the road.

A heavy knot formed in Ragen's throat as he looked at the burned-out house. The Boggers had thrown water on the last embers, and the whole yard was filled with the acrid stink of fire and blood.

It was a stench Ragen was sorry to say he knew too well. Every Messenger did. But no matter how many times it happened, it was never something you got used to.

Like ghosts, he could see the Damaj family running through the yard and taking ease on the porch, enjoying the long summer evenings.

Now the Boggers were laying their few remains on a bonfire pallet under the supervision of the local Tender, who was struggling to piece the bodies together enough for a proper pyre.

It was too much. Ragen stumbled down from his horse and bent almost double, putting his head between his knees, struggling to breathe.

He felt a hand on his shoulder, and looked up at Tender Heath's kind gaze. There were tears in Heath's eyes, too.

Ragen swallowed hard, his voice coming out a croak. 'Anyone get out alive?'

Heath gave a tired shrug. 'Only found pieces enough for one twin, but it might be parts from two for all I know.'

Ragen nodded. 'Couldn't tell where one of those ripping boys ended and the other began even when they were alive.'

Heath grunted, as close to a laugh as one could get with such dark humour. 'No sign at all of Briar.'

Ragen looked up at that. 'Have you organized a search?'

Heath nodded. 'Got folk searching the bog, but . . .' He shrugged. 'Boy was small. Good-sized demon could have swallowed him whole.'

It was true enough, but Ragen wouldn't let himself believe it. Relan was his friend, and if two of his sons might still be out there, hurt and scared, he owed it to his friend to find them.

'Hold the pyre,' he said. 'Going to have a look myself.'

Heath nodded. 'We'll take the pallet to the Holy House so I can scatter the ashes on warded ground. I can give you till dusk horn.'

The Damaj yard had been churned by the feet of countless Boggers come to help or gawk, but in the garden Ragen found what he was looking for. Footprints. Dawn and Briar, from the look. Dawn had left the boy in the hogroot patch. Smart.

Then she had run back inside to be cored.

Ragen breathed through the tears. Briar had made it out of the house to a safe space, but the heat and smoke must have been terrible. A careful search found where he had stumbled from the garden, running for the refuse cart, and from there, into the bog.

It was an hour before Ragen picked up the trail again, spotting the sugar candies lying in the dirt, covered in ants. Briar's prints were all around the base of the goldwood tree.

'Briar?' he called into the boughs. 'You up there, boy?'

When there was no reply, Ragen sighed, catching the lowest branch and pulling himself up. This would hurt on the morrow.

The hollow in the branches where Briar had spent the night

was easy enough to spot. A twist of corn husk from a sugar candy was stuck to a bed of churned leaves, and the nook stank of hogroot.

He lost the trail from there, wandering for hours in the bog, calling Briar's name. He searched the dump as well, knowing how much time the Damaj boys spent there, but still there was no sign.

The Great Horn sounded, signalling the dusk, and Ragen mounted Nighteye with a heavy heart, riding hard back to the Holy House. If there had been a single sign of the boy since he left the goldwood, Ragen would have set his circles and waited all night, listening for cries.

But it was pointless. Much as it cut at him, Ragen knew the truth. He might have made it further than most, but a boy of six, out in the naked night?

Briar was dead.

Boggers might not visit the Holy House every week, but the whole town would come to pay respects at a funeral pyre, even for a family that had never quite fitted in. They were sombre out of respect, but there were few tears apart from Ragen and the Tender. Only Tami Bales wept openly.

As folk were exiting the service, Masen Bales spat. 'Least I don't owe that mudlover Dawn eight shells any more.' His brothers chuckled.

Ragen took a firm grip on the man's shirt, holding him in place for the punch. He felt a crack, and bits of tooth flew from Masen's mouth.

The other Bales men ran to defend Masen, but Ragen grabbed Masen's arm, ducking into a throw that slammed him into his brothers and brought them all down in a heap.

'You'll pay ten each to the Holy House for their grave marker,' Ragen growled, 'or Creator is my witness, I'll see none of you ever get mail again.'

Marta Speaker was there in an instant. She interposed herself between them, but it was hard to tell whose side she was on, glaring at all the men equally. 'That ent going to be necessary, Messenger.' She looked to the Bales brothers. 'You heard the man. You men can't respect the dead, then go on home and find your purses.'

The men didn't move, and Ragen wondered if pride might demand a battle they were bound to lose. He almost wished they would come at him. A few broken bones would teach them to respect the dead, and remind them they were lucky to be alive.

The other Boggers watched the scene impassively. More than one likely shared Masen's sentiment, but none were stupid enough to cross a Messenger, especially one of Ragen's stature. Fortunes rose and fell on a Messenger's goodwill.

Tender Heath joined Marta, putting his hands on his hips and staring down the Bales men. The flames of the pyre roared behind him, adding a looming presence. Masen's brothers tipped their hats and left on the quick. Masen spat a wad of blood and waved for his family to do the same.

'The Holy House offers you succour tonight, Messenger,' Heath said, when the fire had burned down.

'Grateful, Tender,' Ragen said. 'Got a jug of Krasian spirits I meant for Relan. Be honoured if you'd have a drink with me.'

Heath coughed, looking at the tiny cup in disbelief. 'Hits harder than a pint of my best ale, and tastes like firespit. Drink like this ought to be illegal.'

Ragen chuckled. 'It is. The *dama* will cut the thumbs off anyone caught selling it, and even being caught with some will earn you a whipping.'

Heath shook his head. 'Impossible. Relan said it was a popular drink in Krasia.'

Ragen poured another round, clicking tiny cups with the Tender before they both drank. 'Krasia's just like everywhere else, Tender. Got their holy and their hypocrites. The Evejah says drinking spirits is a sin—'

'Creator forbid,' Heath said.

'—but that doesn't mean everyone listens.' Ragen stared into his empty cup. 'Relan ever tell you why he left Krasia?'

Heath nodded. 'They lock their warriors in a maze full of demons each night, and treat those that flee like refuse. He said you offered something better, and risked your life to sneak him past the gates.'

Ragen laughed. 'That what he told you? Ay, it's true after a fashion, but it puts quite a shine on things. Truer is I'd never seen Relan in my life when I left Fort Krasia that morning. Put hard miles between me and the city till nearly dusk, then unhitched the cart and set up my portable circles.'

He poured two more cups of couzi. 'So I'm starting a fire and putting the kettle on when out of the shadows walks this *Sharum* in full warrior blacks, spear and shield in hand. Scared the piss out of me. Went for my spear, but even after hanging onto my cart axle all day, he picked off my thrusts like I was an apprentice still using a training spear. Don't think I'd have had a chance if he'd been fresh.'

Heath took the offered cup. 'What happened?'

Ragen shrugged. 'He gave me a good whack with the spear that sent me sprawling. Might've killed me if he'd taken advantage, but he just lowered his spear and waited. Realized then he wasn't attacking me, just defending himself. Coreson didn't speak a word of Thesan, but I knew the market pidgin well enough for us to stumble through half a conversation. Begged me to take him north, and we ended up riding together almost three seasons before your pretty Gatherer caught his eye.'

Heath nodded. 'Whole town was in an uproar when they asked me to wed them. Don't think I would have done it if Relan had converted just for her.'

'He was on his way to converting before we were out of the desert,' Ragen said. 'Relan didn't want to die in the Maze, but he wanted to be right with the Creator. You gave that to him. I remember how he cried after you made the signs and blew incense over him.'

Ragen lifted his cup. 'Seemed like every year there were more of them in that little house. And now it's empty.'

'To Relan and the Damaj family,' Heath said as they clicked and drank. He looked at the cup curiously. 'It tastes . . .'

'Like cinnamon,' Ragen agreed. 'Only you've got to be rot drunk to notice.'

Heath stoppered the jug. 'Best leave off a bit, then. Want to keep my wits about me tonight, and blow the horn every hour.'

The Tenders of the Creator lived by the Law of Succour, that said the Holy House must be a place of refuge from the night at any hour. There were few Warders in the world who could match the powerful script Tenders learned as acolytes. Church wards were much harder to draw, but the complex nets were impenetrable, rebounding a coreling's attacks back on them with such force that a determined demon might beat itself to death at the wardwall without ever breaking through.

The path to the front doors was lit with lamplight through the night, to aid those running for succour, and never locked. Tenders lived by simple means, and had little to steal in any event.

The Great Horn was blown each evening an hour before dusk, and again at sunset, to show the way to those in need. If the Tender meant to blow it throughout the night . . .

'You still think Briar might be out there?' Ragen asked.

Heath looked at the clock and pushed unsteadily to his feet. 'When I asked Relan why he was willing to foreswear the Evejah and follow the Canon, he told me, "I see now that if Everam's power is infinite, then even Nie exists only at his sufferance. And so the *alagai* must come at his will. What can this be, save punishment for our sins?"'

Ragen frowned. 'You'll forgive me, Tender, but I've never

held to that. Creator loves us, it's said. What loving being would set the corelings on us?'

'It's a paradox,' Heath agreed. 'One better men than us have argued through the ages. But the Canon and Evejah both agree that the Creator's power is infinite.' He stumbled over to the Great Horn, pausing to wet his lips. 'We live in the real world, and make our choices based on what's in front of us, but we can always pray for a miracle.'

He drew a powerful breath, and blew.

Ragen went hunting for Briar the next day, and the day after that, but he found no further sign. Perhaps the Creator could grant miracles, but if so, he was stingy with them.

Ragen had expected a sense of melancholy when the great walls of Miln finally came into sight, but found his heart lifting instead. Yes, he was leaving the world behind, but maybe Relan had the right of that. His friend had always been devoted to his family first. What better way could Ragen honour him than to stop his wandering and cherish his own family?

He entered the city looking forwards, not back.

He made his way into the warding district where Cob kept his shop, a quick stop before returning home for good. Arlen was polishing his armour when Ragen entered the shop.

'If you paid half the attention to that girl of yours you do to that armour, you'd have her eating out of your hand.'

Arlen looked up smiling. 'If that ent the night calling it dark, dunno what is. Might have more time for Mery if I wasn't waiting on Lady Elissa in your place.'

Just her name sent a thrill through Ragen. 'She is well? The child . . .'

'Looks like she swallowed the base of a snowman,' Arlen said, 'but the Gatherer says everything's sunny.' He turned to give a shout into the back. 'Cob! Ragen's back!'

A moment later, the grizzled old Warder appeared. 'Ragen! How was your last tour?'

'Easy and safe, for my part,' Ragen said.

'Did you make it all the way to the desert?' Arlen asked.

Ragen shook his head. 'Settled for a night on Lookout Hill.'

Arlen's smile soured. 'Been settling for looks too long. Can't wait till I get my licence and can see for myself. Going to go places no Messenger's ever been.'

'You want to be Marko Rover, then?' Ragen said.

Arlen shrugged. 'Every Messenger wants to be Marko Rover.'

'Ay, the boy has the right of that,' Cob said. 'Used to beg the Jongleurs for tales of the Rover when I was a lad.'

Ragen nodded. 'Fair and true. The tales tell of the wondrous places Marko went, but they always seem to leave out the weights his heart brought home.'

'Are you saying it's not worth it?' Arlen asked.

'Creator, no.' Ragen winked. 'I've got letters in my bag from half the Merchants and Royals south of the Dividing, asking for Arlen Bales to take my summer run to Lakton.'

Arlen's eyes widened. 'Honest word?'

Ragen nodded. 'With Count Brayan in your corner after your mad adventure to his mines, Guildmaster Malcum will have a hard time refusing.'

Arlen leapt to his feet with a whoop. It was so unlike the serious boy that Ragen did not know how to react. He looked to Cob, finding the old Warder equally dumbfounded.

'Elissa won't like it,' Ragen said. 'Nor Mery, I imagine.'

'They won't hear it from you,' Arlen said, taking in both men with his gaze. 'Neither of you. I'll tell them when I'm ready.'

Ragen nodded. 'Now all that's left is for me to decide what to do with the rest of my life.'

'I've some thoughts on the matter,' Cob said, 'since you've all but ensured I'm losing my partner.'

4

Mudboy

333 AR Autumn

Mudboy watched the bog demon prowl the refuse mounds from the safety of one of his many hogroot patches.

'Hogroot grows angrily as a weed,' his mother used to say. Simple cuttings grew stalks of their own in almost any soil. In the fertile ground of the dump they spread like firespit, choking out other plants to form islands of safety in the naked night.

The cory sniffed, finding the first rat, blood still warm on its fur. The demon gave an excited croak, catching the rat on a talon and tossing it into its open maw. It bit once and swallowed the creature whole.

Mudboy kept perfectly still. The demon was mere feet from him, but it heard nothing – saw nothing. The hog resin and mud on his clothes blended him perfectly with his surroundings, and the stink of him was enough to turn any demon's nose.

Some cories were content to rise in the same place every night, hunting within a small radius and sinking back down in the same spot at dawn. Mudboy knew the ones in the area, and where they were apt to be found.

Other demons tended to roam, falling back to the Core wherever their wandering left them and rising in the same spot that night. This one had been drifting closer for days. Mudboy had planted clusters of hogroot at every approach, but the dump drew cories like standing water drew skeeters. Cories hungered for human flesh most of all, and the dump was thick with people stink.

Mudboy dug pits, laid tripwires, and even burned hog smoke in its path, but despite his every incentive to hunt elsewhere, the bog demon had got uncomfortably close to the briar patch, his hidden lair. It couldn't be allowed to stay.

The rat had barely been a mouthful, but a few feet away the cory found the next one, and another a few yards from there, leading it inexorably towards the precipice where the waste cart dumped.

Mudboy shook his head. It was the third time this particular demon had wandered into the dump and been lured to the exact same spot. Father said cories had brains as tiny as a shelled pea. He shifted his grip on the old broomstick fitted to the head of his father's spear and slipped his arm into the mended straps of the shield, wondering if this one would ever learn.

Already the bog demon was beginning to stumble. The rats were poisoned with a mix of skyflower and tampweed. A single rat had little effect, but after five it would be clumsy and slower.

Slower, but not slow. Even the slowest, stupidest cory could tear him to pieces if he was not swift and precise. He had seen firsthand what they could do.

You must always respect the alagai, *my son,* father had said, *but you should never be ruled by your fear of them.*

Mudboy embraced his fear and was moving in an instant, swift and silent as a bird. The demon was looking away, and would never know he was there. It would see only the flash of magic as it struck the shield, and then it would be flying over the edge.

But as the demon reached for the final rat, it paused, as if remembering. Mudboy picked up speed. It was smarter than he thought. Next time he would need a new trick.

Even drugged, the demon was fast. Its head snapped around, seeing him coming in time to dig hind claws into the ground, swiping with its front talons.

Unable to stop in time, Mudboy tumbled into a roll, ducking the talons by inches. He pulled up just short of the precipice and turned just as the bog demon hawked and spat.

He ducked behind his shield, but the mucky phlegm spattered off the surface, droplets hitting him on the face and body. He could feel it burning, eating away at his flesh.

Keeping his eyes shut, Mudboy dropped his spear, grabbing damp clumps of soil and rubbing them into his face until the burning cooled. He kept his shield up, but he had lost the advantage, and both of them knew it. The bog demon covered the distance between them in one great hop, landing in front of him with a terrifying croak.

It struck fast, but the blow skittered off the wards on the shield. With his free hand Mudboy reached into his pocket, grabbing a fistful of hogroot powder. He threw it in the demon's face as it inhaled to croak at him again.

The demon choked, clutching its throat, and Mudboy danced around it, putting his shoulder to the shield as he ploughed ahead, knocking it off the ledge.

He stood at the cliff's edge, watching as the demon shrieked and tumbled down the steep, garbage-strewn slope into the bog far below. The slime and muck gave no purchase to the demon's scrabbling talons as it disappeared into the fog.

The fall couldn't do any permanent harm to the demon – nothing could, really – but it got it away from his home, which was all that really mattered. Climbing back up would be all but impossible. The cory would shake itself off and wander into the bog. It might be months before he saw this particular demon again, if ever.

His face was still burning despite the cool mud, and looking down, Mudboy saw droplets of bogspit on his clothes, smoking as they burned. There was a broken half-barrel he used to catch rainwater, and he ran for it, dunking his head and scrubbing away the rest of the muck.

He touched his face, flinching back at the sting.

Stupid, he thought. *Your fault. Careless.*

He'd need to mix a poultice.

When he saw the moon had set, Mudboy lifted the compress from his face, flexing his jaw experimentally to pull at the skin. It was red and raw where the bogspit struck, but the quick application of mud staved off the worst of it. The piecemeal smock of salvaged leather he wore under his clothes was pock-marked with a dozen tiny holes, some burned clear through the thick hide.

His mother would have said to keep the poultice on for the rest of the night, but it was Seventhday, and his mouth watered at the thought of the Offering.

He slipped out of the briar patch, moving the broken table that served as his door just enough to slip out, then pushed it back in place, covering the small entrance in the nook behind the largest of the refuse heaps.

He crouched as he moved, the hogroot tall enough to hide him completely. He broke off a few leaves as he went, crushing them in his hands and rubbing them on his clothes to freshen the scent. The cloth was stained nearly black, as much resin as thread by now.

He stepped around the hidden demon pit, and nimbly hopped over the tripwire, pausing to scan the area from between the stalks before stepping from safety.

No cories.

He made his way down the road, passing many dark and silent cottages – the inhabitants long since asleep. Demons prowled the village, but Mudboy knew their habits, passing largely unnoticed.

The few cories that sniffed the air quickly turned away, often with a sneeze. Hogroot soup, his usual dinner, made even his sweat and breath repellent to the cories. Those few that noticed him tended to leave him alone, unless he was fool enough to get too close.

They were thicker by the Holy House. The yard was lit with lanterns, drawing the demons away from the village proper. Cories circled the edge of the wardwall, occasionally causing a flare of magic as they swiped at it in frustration.

Lone cories kept their distance, but a group could surround him, and they were more aggressive in packs.

But there was bread and ale on the other side of those demons.

You have to be bold, his father said. *When I was in Sharaj, the boy who was too timid went hungry.*

The Tender laid the Offering on the altar at Seventhday service, a loaf warm from the oven on a covered platter and ale still foaming in a lidded mug. Ancient wards of protection were etched into the pewter, guarding gifts of comfort and nourishment to any who might come to the Holy House in search of succour.

After a day, the bread began to harden and the ale was flat, but that first night . . .

His mouth watered again. The bread crust would be crisp, the meat beneath soft and chewy. The ale would tickle his throat with bubbles. The taste of them was the closest Mudboy ever felt to Heaven.

And so he came to the Holy House once a week, if not to pray. His father would have spat at the disrespect, but he was dead and could no longer scold. Mudboy knew the Creator would not be pleased at his theft of the gifts of succour, but what had Everam ever done for him, save take his family away? Bread and ale were poor compensation, but compared to the cold vegetables and raw meat he usually ate, it was a feast worth risking a few cories for.

Mudboy crouched low, circling the wall until he was out of sight of the window. He waited for a gap in the circling demons, then darted in. The wards chiselled deep into the wall made perfect hand and footholds, and he was over it in seconds, dropping down amidst the markers where the Tender buried the ashes of the dead. The lamplight in the yard cast the names etched into the stones in shadow, but Mudboy needed no light to find his family's marker.

Miss you, he thought, running his fingers over the notches he'd made in the stone, one for every winter they'd been gone. There were nine now. The faces of his family were hazy in his mind's eye, but the emptiness of their loss had not lessened.

He kept to the shadows of the markers as he crossed the yard, in case the Tender was secretly watching from another window. In moments he had his back to the Holy House wall, inching his way around to where the wing joined the main structure, forming an L. The low sill of a window on the first floor was perfect to launch himself across to catch the sill of one on the second. As with the outer wall, chiselled wards gave him all the hold he needed to scale the rest of the way to the roof.

The Tender had been trying for years to discover who took the Offering each week. It had become something of a game between them. The Tender had put bells on the doors and windows, but had yet to realize his weekly visitor was using the horn tower at the centre of the peaked roof.

Mudboy paused, looking out over Bogton. The many cottages of the town were dark, but it was a clear night, and in the light of the moon he could see far, all the way to Masen Bales' farm. The old man still owed his family eight shells for Maybell, and Mudboy took it in milk once a week. It wasn't stealing, really, and was a chance for a glimpse of Tami. She got prettier every year. Boys had already come to court, but that was all for now. He could still watch her sometimes, and dream of what could have been.

With a sigh he slipped through the tower door and padded quietly down the steps. His shoes were mismatched, but they fitted well enough, worn and softened with use. There was not so much as a whisper as he passed through the vestry and into the nave.

The lamp at the head of the altar was always burning at night, a guide like those in the yard to those in need of succour. The light struck the altar table and pulpit, casting long, deep shadows for Mudboy to follow to his prize. He kept his eyes on the choir loft where the Tender liked to hide, but there was no sound or sign of movement. The Tender drank ale while he waited, and was usually fast asleep this late.

He lifted the pewter mug first, thumbing open the lid and drinking deeply, letting the bubbles tickle his throat and the alcohol soothe the pain of the night's encounter. Then he reached for the bread tray.

There was a ringing as he lifted the lid. The Tender had affixed a bell underneath, where it could not be seen.

Mudboy's eyes flicked to the choir loft. Nothing. The shadows were just a few feet away. If he was quick . . .

But then the vestry door slammed open, revealing Tender Heath, a look of triumph on his round red face.

They stood frozen for a moment, the Tender's eyes widening from victory to shock.

'Briar?'

5

A Last Run

333 AR Autumn

Ragen rapped on the side of his carriage and Robbert, the guard riding outside, leaned down in his saddle. 'What's the hold up?'

Robbert sat high, looking out over the traffic clogging the streets of Miln. He shrugged. 'Messenger day. Must be some news from the south causing a fuss.'

Ragen hated the carriage. Time was, he would be the one out in the saddle, escorting carriages.

Now I'm the cargo, he mused, looking to the growing belly under his robes. He was fit for fifty-two, but he was nothing like he had once been.

He had prospered beyond his wildest dreams in partnership with Cob, and when the cancer took his friend and mentor, he had taken over the Warder's Guild in a landslide. Worried once about his future on retirement, now he was one of the richest and most powerful Merchants in the city.

At last they made it back to Cob's shop.

Cob's shop. It was legally his now, and Elissa had run it for years, but it was still Cob's shop in his mind, and he had never changed the sign out front stating as much.

Elissa looked up at the ringing of the door's bell, her face brightening into a smile that washed away his melancholy. A Mother now, she could have done anything with her life after she graduated the Mother's School and had her peerage restored.

After years of ignoring them in favour of her sisters, Elissa's widowed mother, Countess Tresha, had begun paying calls again. She wanted Elissa to follow her into politics, and had been stunned when Elissa refused in favour of running the warding business with Ragen.

Seeing the shop empty, Ragen flipped the sign on the door to 'Closed' and went to his wife. He was about to step behind the counter and take her into his arms when there was a pounding at the door. He turned just as it burst open and Derek Gold appeared, looking haggard and out of breath. He still had his armour on, Messenger satchel dusty from the road.

'Derek!' Elissa cried. 'We thought you weren't due back until tomorrow.'

'Cracked the reins to get here early,' Derek said. 'News'll be all over the city tomorrow. Wanted you to hear it from me first.'

Ragen caught the tension in his voice. 'What news?'

'Might want to sit down first,' Derek warned. 'And if you've been saving any Sweetwell poteen, now might be a good time to crack the seal.'

Elissa came out from behind the counter. 'Stop stalling, Derek. What's happened?'

'I've news of Arlen,' Derek said.

Word had reached Fort Miln that Arlen Bales was the Warded Man, but Derek knew him from before. The two had met years ago, back when Derek had been a station watchman for Count Brayan's gold mine, and Arlen an apprentice Messenger. Arlen had returned with Derek in tow, and the man had worked in the warding shop for years before joining the Messenger's Guild. Now Derek worked weekly mail between Fort Miln and Riverbridge.

'What news?' Ragen demanded. 'Is he all right?'

Derek shook his head. 'He fought the Demon of the Desert on a mountaintop. They say he pitched them both over a cliff, rather than lose.'

Ragen flushed. 'They? Who's they?' He knew how quickly rumours could start, and could not believe it.

'Ent just hearsay,' Derek said. 'Count Thamos wrote the account himself. Saw an official copy.'

Ragen immediately looked to Elissa. She thought Arlen as much her child as any she had borne herself. She stood there, silent, numb.

He went to her. 'He'll be all right. There must be some mistake. Arlen's strong. He's smart, he can't . . .'

The words choked off with a sob as the truth hit home. Not even Arlen could leap off a mountain and live to tell the tale.

Arlen was dead. The bravest man he'd ever met. His apprentice. His ward.

His son.

He shook, eyes blurring, but Elissa was there in an instant, holding him steady, gentling his hair with soothing words. He had thought to be strong for her, but it was the other way around.

'I've got to get home,' Derek said, obviously uncomfortable with the display. 'Stasy ought to hear the news as well.' He opened his satchel, leaving a tied bundle of letters on the counter. 'Brought the mail.'

The tears caught up to Elissa that night, after the children were in bed. They had both taken too much wine at dinner, and Elissa cried herself to sleep in Ragen's arms.

Ragen's eyes were dry. Part of him still could not believe he had wept at all. When was the last time he'd shed a tear? He didn't know he still had it in him.

He was angry now, though at whom or what he did not know. His muscles were bunched as if for a fight, but there was no foe, nothing for him to revenge himself upon. Arlen was gone and there was nothing to be done about it.

He lay awake for hours, tossing and turning, but still sleep would not find him. At last he could stand it no more, and slipped out of bed so as not to disturb Elissa.

The halls of his manse were empty so late at night, dark with the shutters closed tight against the chill mountain air. But Ragen had never feared the dark. He drifted along silently in the blackness, trailing fingers lightly along the wall until he reached his office. He went inside and shut the door, then flipped the switch to turn on the lectric lights.

He went to his desk, opening the drawer where he kept the last of the Sweetwell poteen, priceless now that the corelings had taken Sweetwell.

He struck the seal with his knife, cracking the hard wax, and pulled the stopper. Without bothering with a glass, he took a pull straight from the jug.

And coughed, spitting out half the mouthful. Night, he'd forgotten how strong it was!

He took a cup and poured another measure, cutting it with water. It burned on the way down, but left a numbness in its wake. A numbness Ragen hoped would soon spread throughout his body.

He saw Margrit had left the bundle of letters on his desk, and cut the string. A few more cups of poteen and a reading of his investment tallies should be enough to finally put him down for the night.

Ragen sat back in his chair as he thumbed through the letters. Most were the usual business, though a few held more personal correspondence. The seal on one in particular caught his eye. How long since he had thought of Bogton?

He broke the seal, reading:

Messenger Ragen,

Blessings of the Creator upon you. It is my sincere wish this missive finds you in good health.

Out of consideration for your brave concern and pressing need on the night of tragedy, I inform you that Briar Damaj is alive – or was as of a few weeks prior to my writing this, when I caught him stealing the Offering from my altar. He fled the scene, and has not returned since.

The boy was covered in filth, and he stank. I believe he has been living like an animal in the bog, hiding in the muck from hunting demons. I've spent weeks searching for sign of him or his den, but the wetland is vast and treacherous. Last week I stepped in a sinkhole and broke my leg. Forced to abandon my search, I was lucky to make it back alive.

With the Krasian invasion of Rizon and the warnings from the Mistress of the Hollow that further incursion is to come, none of the Boggers will aid in my search for a half-Krasian boy. Half the town is convinced that Relan was a spy sent to mark a path for his desert masters.

Please, Messenger. Briar is alone in the naked night. You and I are all he has left. Any aid you can offer in bringing him safely behind the wards will be returned upon you a hundredfold in Heaven.

In humility,

Tender Heath
Bogton Holy House
Laktonian Ministry
Year 333 After the Return

Ragen read the letter a second time, and a third, but his eyes kept going back to two short sentences.

Briar Damaj is alive.

Briar is alone in the naked night.

The door opened, and Elissa stood there, wrapped in a dressing gown. 'I woke and you weren't in bed.'

Ragen looked at her. 'I need to go to Lakton.'

Elissa blinked, waiting as if unsure if she had heard correctly. When Ragen did not elaborate, she crossed her arms. 'Why?'

It was never a good sign. Elissa could be stubborn as a rock demon when her arms crossed. Ragen held out the letter, steeling himself for the fight to come.

'I have to go,' Ragen said softly when she finished reading.

'Of course you do,' Elissa said.

'I know it seems impossible, a boy surviving the naked night,' Ragen said.

'Arlen did it,' Elissa said.

'Arlen was twice Briar's age, and a fair Warder,' Ragen said. 'And he would have died, if I hadn't found him.'

'So now you need to go and find this one,' Elissa said. 'Old as you are, you think you've time for one last adventure.'

'I won't be in danger,' Ragen said. 'Euchor has built waystations all the way to Riverbridge, and Arlen himself warded my spear. I'll take Derek with me. He'll be happy for the excuse to flee Count Brayan's manse.'

It was true enough. Derek's wife Stasy had managed to keep her peerage despite marrying a Servant on account of her powerful uncle, but while the count accepted the union – and even pulled strings to get Derek respectable work and a rise to Merchant class – both Brayan and Derek were happier when the man was far from Miln.

'I know,' Elissa said.

Ragen's eyes narrowed. 'Why aren't you arguing? Telling me to send someone else? Threatening to leave before I get back?'

Elissa crossed her arms again. 'Because this time I'm coming with you.'

Ragen argued, of course. An endless debate that lasted the two days it took them to prepare for the journey, and right up to the city gates. But the outcome had never really been in doubt. Elissa was resolute, and more, Ragen found he *wanted* her to come. Wanted her to see the wide world that had kept them apart for so many years. Perhaps then she would understand.

But though he wanted Elissa with him, he wanted her safe. He hired a team of guards to dissuade bandits, armed and armoured with no expense spared. He sent word ahead to Euchor's waystations, reserving rooms and supplies. Derek was all too happy to join them, adding another familiar face to the group.

The first night they took refuge at the inn at Harden's Grove. The Grove had a low wardwall to hold out land demons, though wind demons could still swoop into its streets at night. The inn was well warded, but there were occasional cracks and flashes of light as demons tested the forbidding.

Elissa jumped with each flare, and Ragen stroked the spear Arlen had warded for him. It would bite coreling flesh, Arlen had promised, and Ragen knew better than to doubt the man. Part of him longed to put it to use, to kill a demon after a lifetime of hiding behind the wards. A greater part, wiser, hoped he would never have need to put the weapon to the test.

He groaned as he climbed back into the saddle the second day, tugging at his armour.

'Links pinching?' Derek asked.

'More like my gut squeezing,' Ragen said. 'Gained a pound or two since I last wore it.'

Elissa laughed. 'Ay, just one or two. Like me when I was pregnant.'

'Night, I hope it's not that bad,' Ragen said, pulling back smoothly to avoid Elissa's playful smack.

Derek laughed, patting his own slender belly. 'Easy to keep the weight off when you eat road fare most nights.'

'Ay,' Ragen said, 'but you slow down when the years mount, Derek. Fire doesn't burn as hot, but we keep piling the logs.'

It was more than three weeks' travel from Miln to Bogton, even by the fastest route. A part of Ragen had been eager for the journey, eager to escape the confines of Miln. But Ragen found he had not missed many aspects of the road. His thighs screamed, for when had he last spent an entire day in the saddle? Even at the waystations, pallets were hard and foods were chosen more for how long they would last rather than the desires of the palate.

They would have good meals and beds in Riverbridge, and Angiers, but then there would be nights on the open road before they reached the Hollow, and even more before they reached Bogton.

That second day he got one of the first sunburns of his life. It was only then he noticed how white his hands had become. Messenger Ragen's hands and face had been tanned a deep brown, immune to the sun.

But by the third day, Ragen found his legs again. They climbed a hill for vantage, and he leaned back in the saddle, stretching as the duchy spread out before them.

'This, I've missed,' he said.

Elissa gasped at the sight. 'It's beautiful.'

Ragen reached out, taking her hand. 'It's only the beginning.'

'They'll be rising soon,' Ragen said. 'Time to go inside.'

'Inside' was a canvas tent the men had raised. They were south of Angiers now, on the road to the Hollow.

'No,' Elissa said. 'We're no safer in the tent than out here.

I've spent the better part of the last decade learning wardcraft. It's time I saw a demon.'

Ragen could see the tension in her as she paced back and forth, waiting. Her hand were curled fists at her sides. 'It won't be just one. Wood demons rise in numbers near the road, and it won't take them long to find us.'

Elissa stopped pacing. She took a deep breath, scanning the roadside woods as the sun slipped below the horizon and twilight took the world.

She did not have to wait long. The accursed mist began to seep from the ground, thickening and coalescing like a sculptor slapping clay until a recognizable shape began to form.

It was a wood demon, long-limbed with brown armour, knobbed and rough like the bark of a tree. Its talons could be broken sticks on the blunt side, but Ragen knew from experience the other side was sharp and hooked, equally suited for climbing trees and disembowelling prey.

Its snout split open, revealing hundreds of yellow teeth like etching awls, but Elissa met the coreling's eyes, and he swelled with pride. He'd known seasoned Messengers who couldn't abide to meet a demon's stare.

But when the demon sprang, covering the distance between them in an instant and slashing its talons at Elissa, she shrieked and Ragen's heart skipped like a novice on his first overnight.

The blow was stopped cold by the wardnet with a boom and flare that spiderwebbed from the point of impact like a bolt of lightning.

Elissa watched as the wardnet rebounded the energy, throwing the demon off its feet. She gave a sniff, then went into the tent. The coreling, infuriated by the dismissal, hurled itself at the net again and again, but to no avail.

It went on for some time. The first demon had drawn others, and soon a dozen of them lurked nearby, testing the net in turns.

Creator only knew how, but Elissa managed to fall asleep.

Ragen remembered a time when he had been able to do the same, but the memory had given him nightmares since retirement, and now he lay awake, flinching at every blow.

He drifted off a bit before dawn as the demons quieted, only to be woken a short time later by the sounds of the guards breaking camp. Every bit of him ached as he climbed back into the saddle.

They made it to the Hollow not long after, and had two nights of inns before being back on the road. They asked after Arlen – the Hollowers happy to gossip about the Deliverer – but the news was unchanged. Many believed he would return, but none had seen him in the weeks since the battle.

After the sleepless nights on the road, Ragen was tempted to stay an extra day or two, perhaps pay a call on Count Thamos, but the Tender's words stuck in his mind.

Briar is alone in the naked night.

They pressed on.

They were nearing the fork to Bogton when a Messenger came thundering up the road. His horse was lathered with sweat, and there was a wild look in his eyes.

The man pulled up short at the sight of them, taking a long pull of his waterskin. Ragen didn't know him. He'd been too long out of the business.

'In the name of the Dockmasters, I need a fresh mount,' the man said. 'And you need to turn around.'

His tone set off alarms, but Ragen kept his voice calm. 'What's happened?'

'Krasians,' the man said. 'They've taken Docktown. There's a host of refugees fleeing this way, and no telling if the desert rats are in pursuit.'

'Creator,' Ragen said. 'How far?'

The Messenger shrugged. 'Two days. Maybe three. If the *Sharum* are coming this way, believe me when I say you don't want to be here when they arrive.'

Ragen nodded, turning to Derek. 'Give the man a fresh horse.

The rest of you, turn around and head back to the Hollow. I'll meet you there.'

'And where are you going?' Elissa demanded.

'You know where I'm going,' Ragen said. 'Someone needs to warn the Boggers.'

'You're not going alone,' Elissa said.

'No arguments, Elissa,' Ragen snapped. 'I'm not letting you come.'

'Try and stop me.' Elissa yanked the reins, moving her horse out of reach before he could grab them. She was a skilled rider, and there was little hope of catching her if she did not allow it.

'We don't have time for this,' Ragen said.

'Ay, so stop being stubborn and let's go,' Elissa said.

Ragen scowled, but he turned to the guards. 'Robbert, Natan, give the Messenger your horses so he can alternate. Meet us in Bogton. The rest of you are with us.' He kicked his horse, and they set off for the town at a gallop.

Seventhday services were just ending as they approached the Holy House in Bogton. The faithful were spilling from the chapel doors, congregating in the yard to eat and drink and enjoy the sun on the warm spring afternoon.

'Find the Speaker and give them the news,' Ragen told Derek as they rode up to the hitching post. 'Last time I was in Bogton it was a woman named Marta, but that was a decade ago. Take the men with you, and keep things quiet until the Speaker has a moment to think. These people need to evacuate, but panic won't help anyone.'

'Me?' Derek asked. 'Shouldn't you . . .'

'I'm not in the Messenger's Guild any more, Derek,' Ragen said. 'It's not my place, and I have other concerns if I'm going to find Briar before the town's overrun.'

Derek pursed his lips, but he nodded, tying his horse and

signalling the men to follow as he went into the crowd in search of the Speaker.

Ragen saw Tender Heath at the chapel doors, leaning on a crutch as he shook hands and traded smiles with the exiting faithful. His belly had doubled in size since Ragen had seen him last, but he looked healthy still. His hair more dark than grey, his eyes full of life.

Those eyes widened at the sight of Ragen, and the Tender broke off from a grey couple he had been speaking to, turning to greet him. 'Ragen!' He opened his arms. 'Thank the Creator you've come.'

'How could I not?' Ragen said after a crushing hug. He half turned, gesturing to Elissa. 'My wife, Mother Elissa.' He said nothing of the coming Krasians. The Tender would hear of it soon enough, and Ragen meant to be out looking for Briar by then.

Heath bowed as far as his crutch would allow. 'You honour our tiny village with your visit, Lady.'

'Nonsense,' Elissa said. 'The honour is mine.'

'Our sod roofs and mud streets may not impress as the fabled cobble streets of Miln,' Heath said, 'but there are good folk here.'

'If that were true, we wouldn't have needed to come all this way,' Ragen said. 'What good folk leave a boy not yet sixteen to wander the naked night?'

'Ignorant, frightened ones,' Heath said. 'I'm not defending it, but since the Krasians took Fort Rizon, the Boggers have grown distrustful of outsiders.'

'I don't remember them being any better before,' Ragen noted. 'And it's only going to get worse.'

'Eh?' the Tender asked.

'Never mind,' Ragen said. 'Are you positive it was Briar you saw?'

'Creator my witness,' Heath said, using the crutch to step out of the shade of the doorway and into the open sun. 'He's been stealing the Seventhday Offering off and on for years.'

'Years?' Ragen felt a lump of anger welling in his throat. 'Years?! And you write to me now?'

'Peace, Messenger,' Heath said, holding up a hand. 'I wasn't going to write all the way to Miln just to tell you my Offering was going missing. You might have come all this way and discovered it was squirrels.'

Elissa laid her hand over Ragen's and he realized he was clenching it into a fist. He relaxed, breathing deeply.

'Forgive my husband,' Elissa said. 'He has thought of nothing but Briar's safety these past weeks, and is impatient to begin the search. Please go on.'

'There is nothing to forgive.' Heath drew a ward in the air at Ragen. 'Those were words of love for Briar, and will weigh as such when the Creator judges your heart.'

Ragen forced himself to be patient. He had never been religious.

'Been trying to catch the thief for years,' Heath went on. 'Put bells on every door and window, slept on the altar, everything I could think of. But sooner or later I nodded off or turned my back an instant, and the next thing I knew the Offering was gone.'

Heath held up a finger in triumph. 'But then it hit me. I put a bell inside the tray cover. I was hiding in the vestibule, and when I heard the ring I —' he clapped his hands loudly '— pounced! Caught him right in the act. He was filthy, and older, but it was undoubtedly Briar Damaj.'

'How is that possible?' Ragen asked. 'A boy of six surviving a decade in the naked night?'

Heath spread his hands. 'I prayed for a miracle. Perhaps the Creator had one to spare for the poor boy.'

'I seen him, too.' The three of them turned to see the speaker. She was perhaps sixteen summers, still a girl by Milnese terms, but a woman grown out in the hamlets. She was familiar, but Ragen couldn't place her.

'What do you mean, child?' Heath asked. 'Seen whom?'

'Briar Damaj,' the girl said.

'Ay, Tami!' a voice called. Ragen looked up at her family and realized why she looked familiar. Masen Bales still had a gap in his teeth where Ragen had knocked one out.

'Seen him watching me sometimes,' Tami said, 'from across the yard in the hogroot patch.'

Masen stormed over. 'Ay, girl. What the Core you think you're doin', interrupting the Tender when he's with someone?'

'A moment please, Masen,' Heath said. 'Tami was telling us she's seen Briar Damaj.'

'Night!' Masen cried. Tami wilted at the glare he threw her. 'Don't you go spouting that Mudboy nonsense again, girl.'

'You saw him, too,' Tami dared to argue.

Masen shook his head. 'Saw some boy trying to peek as you bent to milk the cow, but he ran off before I got a look at him. Coulda been any of a dozen *living* boys in this stinking town. Sure as the sun wasn't some ripping ghost.'

He looked back at the Tender apologetically. 'Girl told all her friends about the ghost, and now half the kids in town are telling fire stories about having seen the Mudboy.'

'What about the other time?' Tami demanded of her father.

Masen rolled his eyes. 'Here's where she goes completely peat-brained.'

'Why is that?' Heath asked.

Tami looked at her feet. 'Seen him from the window at night, sneaking a cup of milk from Maybell.'

'Half-demon, he'd have to be,' Masen said, 'walking about in the naked night. Either you seen a ghost, or you seen nothing at all.'

Heath coughed. 'Yes, well. Thank you Tami. Good day to you, Masen.' Masen grunted at the dismissal, grabbing Tami's arm and turning to go.

'Just one thing,' Ragen asked, pulling them up short. 'When you saw this boy, which direction were you facing?'

'East,' Tami said. 'Towards the dump road.'

Ragen nodded, producing a gold sun. The coins were common

enough among Miln's upper classes, but in a backwater hamlet like Bogton, half the folk had never even seen gold, and the other half hadn't been allowed to touch. Perhaps it would help as they fled the coming army.

'For your assistance,' Ragen said, handing Tami the coin. She and Masen stumbled away, staring at the coin, dumbstruck.

6

Cories

333 AR Autumn

'This would explain how he kept from being cored,' Elissa said as they approached the Bogton Dump. She waved a hand in front of her nose. 'Demons can't stand the reek.'

While the Boggers were still gathered in the Holy House yard, Ragen and Elissa had asked the local children for tales of Mudboy, paying a silver star for each new one. Most of them were impossible nonsense, but two or three seemed plausible, and on further questioning, Ragen felt sure they had seen . . . something. Something that all credible accounts had coming from the direction of the town dump.

'Reek doesn't cover it by half,' Ragen said, slapping a mosquito on the back of his neck. 'Bog air reeks all by itself. This? This is a work of art. Swamp stink laced with rotting carcass and . . .'

'Something I'd find in a baby's nappy after a night of sick,' Elissa said.

Ragen heaved, but managed to swallow it back down. 'All the more reason we find Briar and get as far from this place as possible. If he's here at all, and this isn't some tampweed tale.'

'You don't believe it?' Elissa asked.

'Heath is famous for drinking his own ale,' Ragen said. 'You can see it in the broken veins of his face. And it was Seventhday, no less. *No hangover like a Tender on Firstday morn*, as the saying goes.'

'The girl swore she saw him,' Elissa said.

Ragen nodded. 'Ay. But it's not odd for a child who's lost a friend to think they see them when they don't.'

'Night, I do that now,' Elissa said. 'Could've sworn I saw Cob on the street in Angiers last week.'

They circled the dump, riding around the junk piles and garbage mounds, getting the lay of the land.

There was vegetation everywhere. Mostly weeds, but also a surprising number of useful plants. At first glance it appeared chaotic, but by the third pass, Ragen began to think it no coincidence. He slipped from the saddle, inspecting the plants.

Elissa followed, squatting to part the fronds so the stalks were visible down to the damp soil. 'They've been cultivated.'

Ragen stood. 'Ay, but that doesn't mean Briar did it. Could have been the refuse collectors or their families. Soil's good here, if you can stand the smell.' They returned to their saddles, circling the area again.

There was a cliff with worn wagon ruts leading to its edge, the place where the rot waste was dumped. The rest of the area was filled with more solid trash, piled into small mountains by generations of waste. At the edge of this was the bog, stretching on for miles into thick and forbidding fog.

'We've never really discussed what we're going to do if we find him,' Elissa said.

'Do you have to ask? We'll take him back to Miln with us.' Ragen smiled. 'It wouldn't be the first time I brought home a stray.'

'What if he doesn't remember you?' Elissa asked. 'What if he doesn't want to go?'

Ragen shrugged. 'Then we drag him for his own good. Can't spend his life living like an animal in the bog.'

There was a rustle in the weeds off to one side, and both of them pulled up short, staring in the direction of the sound. A hogroot patch. The stalks still shook slightly, though there was no breeze.

'Briar?' Ragen called loudly. 'That you, boy?'

There was no response. The stalks settled back in place. But something didn't feel right, and Ragen nudged his horse into the weeds for a closer look.

He was beginning to think he'd imagined the whole thing when there was an explosion of movement as something burst from concealment, a dark blur passing so close his mare gave a great whinny and stood on her hindquarters, kicking the air. By the time Ragen managed to calm her, whatever it was had fled.

'You see that?' Ragen demanded, leaping the horse out of the weed patch. Without waiting for an answer he kicked and rode up one of the more solid mounds of trash, standing in his stirrups for a better vantage.

Elissa was beside him in a moment. 'I only caught a glimpse, but it was too big to be a rabbit, too small for a nightwolf. Saw it dart across the road into the weeds there.' She pointed.

Ragen could see where the weeds were trampled, his tracker's eye following the trail as easily as he found markers on an overgrown Messenger Way. Whatever it was had darted from cover to cover, heading straight for the bog. The fog was still stirring where the thing had disappeared.

Ragen slipped from the saddle, taking his night satchel, spear and shield. 'Stake the horses and put up circles. I'll be back before dark.'

Elissa pointed to the satchel. 'If you'll be back before dark, why are you taking your weapons and portable circle?'

'Common sense,' Ragen said.

Elissa crossed her arms.

Ragen sighed. 'I'll leave markers. Circle the horses and catch up. We've only got a few hours of sunlight left.'

Ragen smacked another mosquito, biting down the curse on his lips, lest he give away their position with his shout. The trail had not been easy to find, but their quarry was in a hurry, and the muck of the bog left undeniable prints. The shoes had mismatched treads, but they were consistent with a teenage boy.

It still wasn't proof, but Ragen wanted to believe.

'I'll admit I thought Messengering glamorous from the warmth of our manse,' Elissa slapped a mosquito drinking deeply from the back of her hand. 'I was even jealous, some-times, when you talked of cities and sights.'

'It's the glamour that makes the Jongleur's songs,' Ragen said. 'They never add a verse for mosquitoes.'

'Or slogging through muck until your boots are soaked through,' Elissa agreed. 'Feels like I'm walking on two blocks of ice.'

'Head back to the horses and dry off,' Ragen said. 'I'll be along soon.'

'Come with me,' Elissa said. 'We can look more in the morning. No reason to cut it close to dark. If that was Briar, he's got a safe place to hide for the night, or he wouldn't have lasted this long.'

A fat mosquito landed on Ragen's nose. He struck it instinct-ively, effectively punching himself in the face. Elissa put a hand over her mouth, hiding a smirk. As the pain subsided, Ragen blew out a long breath. 'Ay, maybe you're right. We'll head back, though I'm not convinced the bog demons are likely to be any worse than these corespawned mosquitoes.'

Elissa looked around, amusement fading from her face. 'You *do* know which way is back in all this fog?'

Ragen smirked, pointing. 'I may be fat and grey, but the first thing you learn as a Messenger is to point north even if you're piss drunk and spun in a circle.'

'Charming,' Elissa said.

Ragen started back to their camp, but stumbled as his boot slipped into a sinkhole. He pitched forwards as pain blossomed in his ankle.

'Corespawned ripping demonshit!' Ragen screamed.

Elissa was by his side in an instant. 'Keep calm.' She dug in the mud to free his ankle, but suction held the boot fast. Ragen screamed again as she pulled his foot free of it, hauling him onto a solid mass of relatively dry peat.

Ragen took a deep breath, flexing the foot experimentally. The dull, throbbing pain flared again with the movement, but everything moved as it was supposed to. 'I don't think it's broken. Find something to bind it, and I should be able to limp back to camp.'

The words had more confidence than he felt, but Elissa took them at face value, taking the riding scarf from her shoulders and wrapping the ankle tight before it could swell. She dug Ragen's boot out of the muck and he bit down hard on a stick as he pulled it back on. She took the night satchel and his shield, leaving the spear for him to lean on.

He limped on for some distance, but they were deeper in the bog than he realized, and the pain grew with every step. At last he could stand it no more.

'I need a moment to rest,' he said, collapsing onto a rotted stump.

Elissa had given him space for pride, but now she moved in quickly. 'You're bathed in sweat. We need to get rid of that armour.'

Ragen shook his head. 'This was my father's . . .'

'I know,' Elissa put a hand at the nape of his neck, stroking his sweat-slicked hair. 'But he wouldn't want us to die for it.'

Ragen gritted his teeth, but he let her help with the fastenings.

'We can send the men for it in the morning,' Elissa said.

'It'll be rusted by morning,' Ragen said as he dropped the heavy linked shirt into the muck. 'And I won't ask any of the men to risk themselves looking for it with an army on the way.'

Ragen took a deep breath and leaned on his spear to stand. Admittedly, it was easier without forty pounds of metal on his back. He began to hope they would make it back to camp with time to spare.

But his ankle howled with every step, the pain worsening as it swelled inside the tough leather of his boot. They would have to cut it off.

First my armour, now my favourite boots, Ragen thought. Then he took another step and his ankle gave out completely, pitching him back onto the ground.

Suddenly the boots were the least of his problems. He looked to Elissa, wondering if they would die here, alone in this Creator-forsaken bog, for a boy who might not exist.

He expected to see fear in her eyes, but Elissa only huffed and cast her eyes about, spotting a wide peat flat amidst the endless streams of the bog. She nodded in satisfaction, and moved to Ragen, putting his arm around her shoulders.

'What are you doing?' Ragen asked.

'You're not going to get much further on that ankle, and I can't carry you,' Elissa said. 'I'll help you to that flat, and then set up the circle around us.'

'You could—' Ragen began.

'I'm being patient with you Ragen,' Elissa said, 'but Creator my witness, if you so much as hint that I should leave my injured husband in the swamp to try and save myself, you'll be wishing the demons got you before I'm through.'

Ragen felt too drained to argue. It took all his energy to stumble to the flat. By the time they made it, he was leaning almost his full weight on her, but Elissa bore it without complaint, setting him in the centre of the flat and taking out his emergency circle. It would be a tight fit, but enough to ward off the demons for the night.

The ground was uneven and damp, hardly ideal, but Elissa moved with assurance, laying the circle. Ragen managed to pull himself into a sitting position at its centre and started work building a fire.

It was going to be a long night.

Ragen stared into the gloom. The light filtering through the fog was dim now, the shadows long and deep. If the sun had not dipped completely below the horizon, it soon would.

'I've done the best I could,' Elissa said, coming over to him. The portable circle was ten feet in diameter, but the island of peat wasn't quite so large and sloped sharply on one end.

While Elissa worked to lay the circle, Ragen cut blocks of peat for her to use in keeping the wardplates level with one another. Several rested on little pillars of the packed moss. Two stood in a stream like bridge supports. Another sat upon a sculpted ledge that hung precariously over a sinkhole. Others, planted on even ground, had muddy water welling up around them.

Individually, the problems were minor, but a series of subtle shifts in alignment could play havoc with a portable circle. The wards would still function, protecting their immediate vicinity, but Ragen and Elissa's lives depended on the web the magic wove as the wards linked together, their lines of power forming a dome of protection around them.

'You did masterfully,' Ragen said. 'If we get back to Miln, you'll receive a medal from the Warder's Guild.'

Elissa smirked. 'I hear the Guildmaster gives those to all the Warders he sleeps with.'

'Only the ones that save my life.' Ragen got slowly to his feet. The rest had done him some good, as had the pinch of bitter stiffroot powder he had washed down. The pain was numbed, and the swelling less, now. He was in no position to run, but their lives might depend on swift action the first time a demon tested the wards.

There would be holes in the net, but there were too many factors at play to guess them precisely. But when a coreling struck the circle, the wards would leach some of the creature's magic and there would be a flare of power through the net.

It would be gone in an instant, like lightning forking in a cloudy sky, but it would be enough for them – and the demons – to see the gaps.

If the gaps were small, or easily defensible, they would see the dawn. If not, Ragen would get to put his warded spear to use, fending the demons off until Elissa could adjust the plates.

'Any minute, now,' he said.

Elissa nodded, and again Ragen marvelled at the steel in her eyes. He had thought just the sight of a demon would be too much for her, but she was as calm as any Messenger.

The eye in Ragen's mind opened, flashing images of a lifetime on the road together, instead of countless months spent apart. A few other Messengers did it, but Elissa had been royal born, and it had been unthinkable.

His eyes began to tear, thinking of all those wasted years. Elissa saw and brushed them aside with a gentle hand. 'It will be all right. A year from now we'll be back in the warding shop, bickering over how I mother poor Briar.'

He smiled, loving her more than he could say.

But then a bog demon came hurtling out of the fog, and the net flashed to life. Elissa's eyes snapped to the net, searching for gaps, but Ragen's attention was held by the demon. The coreling should have been thrown back by the rebounding magic, but it wasn't. Its claws whined across the wardnet with the sound of a thousand fingernails on slate, magic sparking and crackling in their wake.

'The whole circle's weak,' Elissa said. The net remained

illuminated like the filament of a lectric bulb while the demon touched it, reflecting brightly off the surrounding fog.

They scanned the lines quickly, finding several gaps. One would allow a coreling to tunnel under the circle – easily done in the soft peat – but demons were not known for their cleverness, and might miss it.

Most of the others were too small for a demon to fit through, but with the clawing bog demon keeping the net illuminated, there was a map to the large ones every coreling in the area could follow.

The biggest danger was above their heads. The web should have spun a dome of protection over them, but with so many of the plates out of alignment, it veered at angles, sometimes inwards, sometimes out. The result was a jagged gap two feet wide practically right above them.

'Ragen!' Elissa snapped him out of contemplation, pointing.

Two more bog demons emerged from the glowing mist. Overhead there was a shriek. The flashing wardlight had caught the attention of wind demons, as well.

One of the demons struck at the wardnet, but the plates there aligned properly. It was thrown back, leaving a deep dent in the peat a dozen feet away.

Ragen smirked, but it was short-lived as the other demon's claws skidded across the forbiddance, catching fast on an open seam. Elissa shrieked and leapt back as it thrust a long, spindly arm through the gap, talons closing mere inches from her face.

But the flaring lines of power remained impassable, and the demon was held fast at the shoulder. It croaked in pain as magic buzzed and crackled, sending shocks through its body, but with human prey in sight it did not give up, straining against the magic with every fibre of its being.

A ten-foot circle was large enough if it was working properly, but if demons could reach at them from all sides, the safe space shrank to almost nothing.

'It's stuck,' Elissa said, catching her breath. 'It won't get through.'

'Doesn't matter,' Ragen said. 'This racket will lure every demon for miles. They'll break the circle with sheer weight of numbers.'

'What can we do?' Elissa asked. 'I can't adjust the plates with it swiping like that.'

Ragen lifted his spear, meeting the bog demon's huge, lidless eyes with a cold stare. The coreling clawed the air impotently, struggling to reach him. 'I'll just have to ask it to quieten down.'

In one smooth movement, he stomped forwards, thrusting his spear. His ankle exploded with pain, but it was a distant thing, like a flash of light in the distance. In his mind, there was only the demon and the spear.

The wards formed an impenetrable barrier for the demon, but for the spear it was only air. A bog demon's tough, slimy skin could turn almost any thrust, but the wards Arlen had carved on the spearhead flared, and it punched clear through the demon's chest.

Power shocked up the shaft and into his arm, jolting him with magic. Arlen had spoken of the effect, but Ragen had never felt it himself.

The tales failed to do it justice. Strength surged through Ragen's muscles, blasting away fatigue. The pain in his ankle faded, allowing him to put weight on it again.

He understood now Arlen's addiction to fighting demons. The demon croaked in pain, flailing at him, but Ragen was fast and agile like he had never been, easily dodging the hooked claws. With the magic coursing through him he felt euphoric, immortal. They would survive the night, even if he had to kill every coreling in the bog.

It was with reluctance that he tried to pull the spear free. The weapon was caught fast, but Ragen worked his powerful arms, slamming it into the wardnet over and over until the spearhead popped free and the demon fell back, dead.

Night, Ragen said, feeling his stomach drop. *I just killed a ripping demon.* Relan had told him the *dal'Sharum* did this every night, but until this very moment, a part of him had not believed it.

The commotion had drawn more of the creatures. They quickly surrounded the weakened circle, jostling one another for position as they tested the wards.

One found another gap and stuck an arm through, but before Ragen could react, two of its fellows leapt on it, killing the demon and gnawing its arm until one end dropped lifelessly into the circle.

Elissa turned from the sight, and even Ragen felt his stomach churn. The two demons then turned on each other, fighting for access to the gap in the wards. Two other demons found open seams, and now there were grasping talons on all sides.

Ragen snatched up his shield and set his feet, thrusting into any demon that got too close to a gap. The wards on the spear were hungry, tearing into coreling flesh with a sizzling spray of ichor, illuminated in the wardlight. But not every blow was a killing one, and the magic jolting through him was just a taste of what coursed through their veins. Many fell back only to recover a few moments later and return to the press.

He moved back to the tiny island of safety at the circle's centre to catch his breath. Ragen still felt strong, the pain in his ankle now just a dull throb, but the euphoria had faded and reality set in. He would fight to his last breath, but there were too many demons, and likely more on the way.

They were going to die.

Unable to get close to the crowded circle, one bog demon leapt atop the back of another and sprang high, hooked claws catching the edge of the jagged gap in the wards above. Magic spiderwebbed through the air as it dragged itself to the opening. The demon coughed a thick spray of bogspit into the circle as it readied itself to pounce.

Ragen wrapped an arm around Elissa, pulling her close as

he threw up his shield. There was a thump and crackle as the glob of bogspit rebounded off the wards, spattering in every direction. He swept the shield aside, hurling his spear at the demon before it could drop into the circle.

The moment the weapon left his hand, Ragen knew it was a mistake. The spear took the coreling full in the chest, but the demon took the weapon with it as it fell back, landing dead a dozen feet from the circle.

Bogspit droplets clung to their clothes like snot, already beginning to smoke and burn, but with talons grasping at them from all around, it was the least of their problems. They huddled close, turning slowly as they hid behind the scant protection of the shield.

The entire wardnet shook. Ragen's tendons clenched as he followed the distortion back to its point of origin. Bogspit had struck the taut rope between the wardplates resting on the pillars in the stream. It was smoking, and any second . . .

The rope snapped, and an entire quadrant of the circle fell away. The corelings tensed their muscles to spring for the gap, fully prepared to claw their brethren out of the way to be the first to enter.

'Get ready to run,' Ragen said.

'Run where?' Elissa demanded.

'For the spear,' Ragen said. 'It's our only hope now. I'll shield rush the first to come through the gap, throw it back into the others. That should distract them.'

'I don't know how to use a spear,' Elissa said.

'The point goes in the demon,' Ragen said. 'It's hardly wardcraft.'

The biggest of the demons shoved to the fore of the press, launching itself through the gap. Ragen set his feet, ready to stop it fast with the warded shield, fully aware of the futility of it all.

A sudden roar filled the night, freezing the bog demons in place. Ragen was not reassured. It was a sound he knew well.

The approaching rock demon might keep the bog demons at bay, but only so it could kill them itself.

But what was a rock demon doing in ripping Bogton of all places? They were common enough in Miln, but rock demons needed a large, natural facing of stone to rise to the surface – not something often found in the Laktonian wetlands.

The roar came again, closer, but this time there was something . . . off about it. A resonance he had never before heard in the familiar cry. A reverberation not to be heard in a swamp.

He caught the orange glow of a flame demon in the fog, growing brighter. As if a knot of bog demons and an angry rock weren't enough.

The flame demon charged an active part of the circle, but the coreling was not stopped by the wards as it burst from the fog, mouth glowing with orange flame as it roared.

Ragen and Elissa froze, but the demon swept past them with a trail of choking smoke. It leapt in front of the gap, belching fire and smoke at the confused bog demons.

'That's not a demon,' Elissa said.

Ragen's eyes widened. What he had taken at first for a flame demon was a boy not yet in his full growth, clad in mismatched rags and a thick coating of swamp muck. On his back was a round *Sharum's* shield and in one hand he held a bundle of hogroot stalks, the end burning with an oily, pungent smoke. He swept the torch back and forth, creating a wall of fumes. In his other hand he held a sheet of bark curled into a cone. As Ragen watched, he put his lips to the small end, letting out an impressive imitation of a rock demon's roar.

The bog demons began to choke, and when the boy backed towards them, they did not immediately follow.

'Cories hate hog smoke,' the boy rasped, never taking his eyes off the demons drifting through the fog and smoke. Words were awkward on his tongue, and Ragen had to strain to understand. 'Makes 'em cough n' slosh up. Watch and follow me.'

If there had been any doubt this was Relan's son, it was gone in an instant as the boy began to do the rocking dance his *dal'Sharum* friend used to confuse corelings. Step to the right, step to the left . . . Half a dozen bog demons turned their heads back and forth in sync with his movements.

Ragen knew which direction the boy was headed long before he started moving. He took Elissa's hand, and like strangers joining together in the steps of a familiar dance, they matched Briar's calm, deliberate strides, four to the left, four to the right. The boy dropped the burning hogroot, obscuring them in the smoke as they walked six steps to the left, counting breaths. On the third, they broke into a run together. Ragen snatched up his spear as they ran past, handing off the shield to Elissa.

They quickly lost sight of the knot of bog demons, Briar leading them on a twisting path through the trees. The abrupt halts and sudden changes of direction seemed random at first, but Ragen was a pathfinder, and soon realized they were travelling a prepared route. A fallen tree, its roots reaching high to block out the moonlight, hid a change of direction. The shallow stream they splashed along washed away tracks and scent. Hunched, a low rise hid them almost completely for a hundred yards.

Ragen caught the scent of the dump well before it came in sight. They had come full circle. He'd been a fool to follow Briar into the bog. The boy had purposely led them away from his lair and left them lost in the swamp. If they'd only just waited . . .

'Look out!' Elissa cried, throwing up his shield. There was a flare of magic and she was knocked into him by the rebound. They went down with a splash into the reeds and mud.

Upside down amidst the tumble, Ragen caught sight of the charging swamp demon, a larger, deadlier cousin to the bog. It was low to the ground, with knobbed scales and short, stubby limbs ending in long, hooked claws perfect for climbing trees.

A swamp demon's snout could bite a man from head to crotch, its tail a heavy lash that could shatter a wooden fence.

Dizzy and with mud in his eyes, Ragen struggled to get his spear up, but Elissa rolled over him, covering them with the warded shield.

The swamp demon struck hard against it, but there was no telltale flare of magic, no rebound that threw the coreling back. Just a high-pitched whine as the demon clenched its talons, tearing through the steel. The wards on its surface were covered in mud – useless. Ragen peeked over the edge at the demon's gaping maw and immediately wished he hadn't.

But then a small gourd struck the shield, shattering and sending a cloud of hogroot powder right into the demon's open mouth. Ragen's eyes teared and he sneezed, but it was far worse for the demon. It fell onto its back, choking.

Briar appeared again, helping them to their feet. Twisted and useless, Elissa left the shield in the mud next to the demon as it convulsed, retching a vile mix of stomach fluids and bogspit onto itself.

'Cory will be up quick,' Briar said in his animal rasp. 'Need to get to the briar patch.'

Ragen nodded, though he had no idea what the boy was talking about. He and Elissa followed as quickly as they were able as the boy darted into the mounds of the dump.

Behind, he heard the demon hiss and scrabble to its feet. His ankle was screaming again, his limp getting worse with each step. Elissa clutched him, taking more and more of his weight. Back to using his spear as a crutch, they ran like they meant to take a ribbon in the three-legged race at a Solstice festival.

But the demon ran faster, stub legs moving at terrifying speed. It closed, and Ragen knew they would not make it wherever the boy was leading before they were overtaken.

Briar saw it, too. He dropped back beside Ragen, pointing to a thick hogroot patch by one of the refuse mounds. 'There. Don't stop.'

With that, he stopped short, giving a cry to get the approaching demon's attention. No imitation demon cry, this was the cry of a human child. Innocent. Vulnerable. For what could get a coreling's attention more than that?

The sound tore at Ragen, but he limped on. By all rights the boy should be terrified, clinging to Ragen for leadership, but Briar spoke with the assurance of a Messenger speaking to travellers on their first overnight, and Ragen found he trusted him.

Elissa was half-dragging him now, supporting him as he put one pained foot in front of the other towards the safety of the hogroot patch. But Ragen's eyes were not on the destination. He watched the demon spot Briar and hiss, giving chase. Focused on the prey at hand, it ran right past Ragen and Elissa, up the hill and away from them.

Ragen remembered the hill. It ended in the steep precipice where the town dumped its rot waste. If Briar didn't change course soon, he would be trapped. The swamp demon saw this, too, putting on a burst of speed.

The sight was obscured as Ragen and Elissa stumbled into the hogroot patch. They stopped, watching from between the fronds.

It was too late. Silhouetted in the moonlight, they watched as the demon crashed into Briar, taking both of them over the edge.

'Briar!' they screamed in unison.

The demon dropped away, croaking as it tumbled down the shit- and garbage-covered slope, but Briar's silhouette hung against the moon, then swung back to the ledge. Ragen could see the vine now, hung from a tree branch extending over the precipice. Briar had lured it there and tricked it over the edge.

'Night,' Elissa said.

Briar raced back to the safety of the hogroot patch, leading the way to a broken table leaning against the refuse mound. He pulled it aside, revealing a narrow opening. Elissa went in first, tugging Ragen along as he crawled inside. Briar came last, pulling the table back into place.

It was pitch dark in a space barely long enough for Ragen to lay prone. With his shoulder pressed against one wall, Ragen could easily touch the other, and even on his knees he had to duck his head. This was where Briar slept all these years? In a tiny dark hole beneath a mound of garbage?

Elissa shivered. 'Colder than it is outside.'

'No flue,' the boy said. 'Draughty.' An orange glow lit his face as he blew a small coal to life on a pair of rusty tongs. He cradled the tiny light in his hand as he took it to the kindling laid in the fireplace. Soon a warm fire was burning, casting a flickering light over Briar's dark hole.

They appeared to be underneath an old cart, its belly their roof. The back wheels were gone, but Briar had salvaged boards to prop the axle. The spokes of the front wheels formed little shelving nooks the boy had dug into the garbage mound. Ragged blankets lined the floor, and the walls were salvaged wood, cracks carefully filled. One wall was an old front door. The other was made of a barrel, part of a table and a dresser with mismatched drawers. There looked to be a working half-door on the far end.

More than one entrance, Ragen noted. *He's smart.*

The walls were lined with little nooks. Some held a shiny bit of stone or glass, a bright feather or mended wooden toy. Elissa found a tiny rag doll amidst the blankets, stitched together from mismatched bits of refuse. Briar growled and snatched it from her, clutching it protectively, and Elissa stifled a sob.

Ragen shifted, and his arm struck the wall, causing a blast of pain. He groaned.

Elissa was holding the arm in an instant, pulling the torn sleeve aside to find a row of claw marks. The wound stank, and Ragen wondered if he would lose his arm before this was done. He reached for his herb pouch, but it was gone from his belt, lost somewhere in their desperate flight.

Briar handed Elissa a cloth, pointing to the barrel wall. 'Water.'

She nodded, finding a spigot and fresh water within. As she cleaned the wound, Briar reached into one of the spoke-shelves, taking out a mortar and pestle. Ragen recognized it instantly. Fine polished marble, he had bought the item in Miln, a wedding gift for Dawn.

As they watched in wonder, Briar began cutting herbs with a bent, wrap-handled knife. Ragen had the Gatherer's art enough to know Dawn had taught the boy well. Briar packed the wounds with a pungent hogroot paste and produced a bent needle he passed through the fire carefully before stitching them shut.

'Thank you,' Ragen said.

'Not taking me away,' the boy rasped. 'Won't let you.'

'We're not—' Elissa began.

'Heard you,' Briar cut her off, turning his glare on Ragen. 'Drag, you said.'

Ragen took a deep breath. He could feel the tension in the boy's fingers as he worked. If he said the wrong thing, Briar would likely be out the door in an instant, and Creator knew if they'd ever find him again.

'Do you remember me?' he said at last. 'I was a friend of your father.'

The boy's eyes flicked over Ragen, the whites stark in the centre of his stained and muddy face. 'Messenger. Brought candy.'

Ragen nodded. 'I owe your father my life. Promised to look after you, if anything happened to him.'

'Don't need looking after,' the boy said.

Ragen nodded. 'Ay, you're your own man. But I want to be your friend, if you'll let me.'

'Don't have friends,' the boy said. 'No one wants Mudboy. Throw rocks. G'way, Mudboy! Getcher stinky hands off, Mudboy!'

Ragen shook his head. 'That's not true, Briar. I'm your friend.' He gestured to his wife. 'Elissa, too. Tender Heath, and Tami Bales. They asked us to find you.'

Briar's eyes widened. He said nothing, but Ragen knew he had found a chink in the boy's armour. 'She's worried about you, Briar. We all are.'

Briar shook, looking down to hide a choked sob. Ragen started to reach for him, but the boy glared at him, and he checked himself.

'Don't know what I done,' he said. 'Everam's punishing me. Don't deserve friends.'

'Nonsense,' Elissa said. 'What could you possibly have done?'

Briar's muddy face scrunched up, and this time he couldn't choke down his sobs. He began weeping openly, and when Ragen reached for him again, he gave only token resistance. The boy stank of filth and hogroot, but Ragen held him as gently as he did his own infant son.

'Din't share,' Briar said, when his convulsions began to fade. 'Din't listen.'

He began weeping again. 'Din't remember to open the flue.'

Ragen stared into the small fire, thinking back on the burned-out husk of the Damaj family home. In an instant he understood.

Creator.

'Wasn't your fault, Briar,' he whispered. The boy gave no indication that he'd heard, but his sobs eased after a time, and at last he fell asleep.

Ragen woke with a start, alone in the tiny den. Panic shocked through him, fearing that Briar had run off again, gone like a wisp of dream. 'Elissa!' he called. 'Briar!'

He needn't have feared. They were waiting just outside the hogroot patch, Briar peeking into the pan as Elissa fried breakfast over a small fire. Nearby lay the portable circle they had lost in the swamp, the plates cleaned and the broken rope mended with stout cord.

'Glad to see you back among the living,' Elissa said. 'Briar and I have been up for hours.'

'We have to go,' Ragen said. 'The sooner, the better.'

Briar shook his head. 'No go. Home.'

'Men are coming,' Ragen said. 'Men like the ones your father left the desert to escape.'

Briar nodded. '*Sharum*. Seen them.'

'Where?' Ragen demanded. 'How many?'

'Two,' Briar said, holding up a pair of fingers. 'In woods, watching'

'When?' Ragen said.

Briar shrugged. 'Firstday?'

Ragen spat.

'What is it?' Elissa asked.

'If they had scouts here a week ago . . .'

The sound of galloping hoofbeats cut him off. Ragen looked up to see Derek riding hard their way. He was clad in his armour, but the helmet was missing, and there was blood in his hair.

Derek rode right up to them, pulling up hard. The horse was still rearing and kicking off its momentum when he vaulted from the saddle. 'Thank the Creator you're all right. We need to leave. Now.'

'What's happened?' Ragen said.

'Krasians,' Derek said. 'Advance guard rode in this morning to sack the town before refugees could succour there.'

'Night,' Ragen said. 'How many?'

'A score at least, all mounted on big mustang,' Derek said. 'We tried to help the Boggers fight. Had them outnumbered three to one . . .' He swallowed. 'They killed Robbert and Natan. Broke Stane's leg.'

Ragen nodded. The Boggers were brave, but they were no fighters. But Krasian warriors . . . that was all they did. The town was lost. 'Where are the others?'

'Hiding in the bog with some of the townies,' Derek said. 'I came to find you and bring you there. If we can keep off the road for a few miles, we should be able to get them to the Hollow.'

'How did you get away?' Ragen asked.

'They were after us but their captain blew a horn and called them back,' Derek said. 'Seemed more interested in plunder and the Holy House than killing or taking prisoners.'

'The Holy House?' Elissa asked.

'Krasians are fanatics,' Ragen said. 'What they do with the townsfolk will depend on the mood of their Kai, but Tenders are heretics – an affront to Everam. They'll claim the Holy House for the coming *dama*, and kill Heath, if they haven't already.'

'Creator,' Elissa said.

'We have to go,' Derek said again. 'Now.'

Ragen nodded. There was nothing else they could do. 'Let's be quick about it. Last thing we want is another night in the ripping bog.'

He turned to Briar. 'You'll need to come with us. It's not safe here.'

But the boy was gone.

Briar's heart thudded in his chest as he raced through the bog. He saw villagers fleeing through the bog, and could guess well enough where they would gather. The *Sharum* would have to give up their horses to follow. Even their scouts had avoided the bog.

None of them noticed his passing, too concerned with themselves. All the Boggers knew the mire, but none so well as Briar. There were infinite places to seek cover while moving at speed.

There were horses and men in the Holy House yard as Briar scaled the wall and dropped among the grave markers. *Sharum* warriors watching with hard eyes as Boggers, eyes down, piled plunder to one side of the yard – food and livestock, mostly.

There was a crash from inside the house, and two *Sharum* came out, carrying the Offering table. This they hurled into a pile with other broken symbols of the Creator. They seemed intent to gut the place, save for the barrels of Heath's ale. These had been carefully set aside and tapped, warriors drinking heavily as they supervised the beaten Boggers surrendering their possessions.

One of the *Sharum* whipped his spear into the back of Aric Bogger. 'Hurry up, *chin*, or you'll go on the fire, as well!'

The other *Sharum* laughed. It had been many years since Briar last heard the language of his father, but he understood enough of their words to fill him with dread.

Not waiting to be noticed, Briar darted through the graveyard to the Holy House wall, climbing quickly to the roof. There was a Krasian in the horn tower, spear and shield leaning against the rail as he held a slender tube to his eye, looking out over the town.

The Watcher did not see or hear Briar as he slipped over the rail behind him, but the smells that hid and protected him at night in the bog did the opposite here. The warrior sniffed, turning just in time to catch the butt of his own spear between the eyes.

The seeing tube fell with a crack, but the warrior rolled, controlling his fall. Before he could recover himself, Briar hit him again. He swung the spear like a club, beating the man about the head until he fell still.

Briar froze, listening, but it seemed none had heard them. He took off the stained and reeking rags he wore, putting on the *Sharum's* blacks before creeping down the steps into the Holy House.

He wanted to pull up the veil to hide his face, but his father's voice came to him, recounting stories of fabled *Sharum*.

No warrior hides his face in the day.

He left the veil down, simply tilting his face towards the wall as a warrior stumbled past carrying an ornately carved chair.

The man barely gave Briar a glance, nodding and grunting as he went about his business.

There were others, but after years of hiding from the Tender as he made for the Offering, Briar knew the halls of the Holy House as well as he knew the briar patch. He moved unseen, searching until a cry of pain led him to the vestry.

Peeking into the room, Briar saw Tender Heath tied to a chair as two *Sharum* stood over him. Both wore black, but one had a white veil about his neck, the other a red. Kai and Drillmaster. The leaders.

Heath's face was swollen, streaked with sweat and blood. His head lolled to the side, eyes closed, panting. His leg was still in a cast from his fall in the bog.

The Drillmaster wiped blood from his fist on the Tender's robe. 'Do we take him to the *dama?*'

The Kai shook his head. 'He knows nothing. Kill him, and we will stake his body in the yard as a lesson to the *chin*.'

The Drillmaster nodded, producing a curved knife, but Briar was already moving. Before the man could take two steps towards the Tender, Briar drove his stolen spear into his back.

The other warrior whirled with a shout, but Briar reached into his robe, clutching a fistful of hogroot powder and hurling it into the man's face. The powder would not affect a human the way it did corelings, but Briar knew from experience how the tiny particles could irritate the eyes.

As the *Sharum* clawed at his face, Briar ducked behind his shield, rushing forwards and knocking him into the wall. He groaned and pushed back, so Briar took a quick step back, then drove forwards again. He broke the press again, cocking back and hitting the Kai in the throat with the edge of his shield. The warrior dropped to his knees, gasping, and Briar took the heavy shield in both hands, bringing it down on the back of his head.

The Kai dropped to the floor and Briar snatched up the knife, cutting the Tender free.

'Who?' Heath asked. One of his eyes was swollen shut, and he had to turn his head for a good look. 'Briar?'

Briar nodded. 'Need to get to the bog. Others hiding there. Krasians won't follow.'

Tender Heath allowed himself to be hauled to his feet. Briar gave him one of the warrior's spears to use as a crutch as they made for the Holy House's back entrance.

'What of the demons?' the Tender asked. 'How will we survive when night falls?'

Briar smiled. 'Cories are easy to hide from.'

'Look! The Tender!' a woman cried.

Ragen looked up, seeing Tender Heath stumbling into camp. His face was bruised and puffy and he leaned heavily on Briar. The boy was clad in Krasian black, but he had discarded the turban and his young, filthy face was unmistakable.

To Ragen.

'And one of them corespawned desert rats!' Masen Bales cried. He and his remaining brother raised their heavy peat spades, freshly inscribed by Elissa with Arlen's fighting wards.

'He's not one of them!' Heath cried, holding out an arm and stepping in front of Briar as several Boggers, led by Masen, moved in. 'This is Briar Damaj! He rescued me from the Holy House!'

'Move aside, Tender,' Masen said. 'Everyone knows those mudskins were spies for the invasion.'

'They know it because you've been telling it to everyone who stands still more than a minute,' Heath said. 'Without a lick of evidence, I might add.'

Ragen shoved through the press to stand with them. 'Briar had nothing to do with the invasion, Masen. He was with us when it happened. He only left when he heard Heath was taken.'

'Then why's he dressed like them?' someone in the crowd demanded, the question echoed by others.

Briar was taut, ready to fight or flee. Ragen expected Masen would quickly regret it if he charged, but there were too many Boggers for them to fight, even as Derek, Elissa, and his remaining men joined them.

'Stole clothes,' Briar rasped. 'To sneak.'

Masen turned and raised his voice to address the crowd. 'Don't be fooled by the Mudboy's lies! He and his paved the way for this. This is the Creator's punishment for accepting that heathen Relan!'

'What nonsense!' Heath cried.

'Nonsense, is it?' Masen demanded. 'Whole town went to the Core when that desert rat showed up. And now we got their kind running wild through town doing Creator knows what!'

There were nods and shouts of agreement from the crowd. Ragen tightened his grip on his spear as Masen pointed the sharp edge of his peat spade at Briar.

'Now you folks get out of the way,' he said, 'and let us skin the mud off that little traitor.' The men in the crowd tensed, readying to close in.

'What in the Creator's name is the matter with all of you.' a high voice shouted, cutting through the din. All eyes turned to Tami Bales, striding between her father and Briar.

Masen balled a fist. 'Girl, you get . . .'

Tami ignored him, addressing the Boggers instead. 'You should be ashamed of yourselves! The Damajes never did a corespawned thing but right by this town, and all we gave them was spit. Now you'll turn on the Messenger who's to guide us to safety, just for a taste of desert blood?'

Masen's scowl only deepened, but the other townsfolk were shifting and looking at their feet now, unsure. He reached out to grip her by the hair, but she stepped back smoothly, delivering a resounding slap to his face.

'Night, Da,' Tami said. 'What would Mum say if she saw you acting like this?'

Masen stood dumbfounded, and as his passion died, the other men took the cue and backed away. Soon it was just the Bales brothers standing alone before Briar, Ragen and his men, and their enthusiasm evaporated with their support.

'Ent going anywhere with that Messenger,' Masen said at last. 'Bogton's my home. Ent leaving it to the desert rats.' None of the Boggers looked ready to lift their weapons again, but there were murmurs of agreement from many.

'You don't need to, Masen,' Heath said loudly, though his voice was dry and hoarse. 'Shepherd Alin of Lakton's been putting a plan in place since Rizon was taken. There's a monastery by the lakeshore with strong walls and a rocky bluff on three sides. The Tenders who've survived the raids will be leading their flocks there. Briar and I are going there, to join the resistance.'

He looked out at the Boggers. 'Families will reunite there, and book passage to Lakton, where the desert dwellers cannot reach. But it is a hard road through the wetland. It may be safer and easier to go with the Messenger. It's a decision each of you must make on your own.'

The Boggers made it quickly, their decision unanimous. They would make for the monastery.

Tami went with her father and uncles as they turned and rejoined the others, but glanced back at Briar as she did. The smile she flashed seemed to strike the boy as hard as the slap she gave her father.

He'll never come to Miln with us now, Ragen thought, but he found he was smiling, too.

He looked at Elissa, who nodded her assent, and turned to Heath. 'I know the monastery. Been more than twenty years, but I can find it again. We'll see you there, and then take Messenger Ways north to avoid the Krasians.'

Ragen looked at Briar. 'The Laktonians will need Messengers

in the coming years, Briar. One who can move through the bogs at night, pass for Krasian, and understand the tongue could mean the difference to the resistance.'

'Father . . . Messaged with you?' The words still fought with his tongue, but they were getting clearer.

'He did,' Ragen said. 'Learned the craft quickly, and could have been great, if he hadn't fallen in love with your mother.' He laid a hand on Briar's shoulder. 'But you, Briar asu Relan, will be even better.'

WARD GRIMOIRE

Introduction

Wards are magical symbols whose origins are lost to history. Long thought to be the stuff of superstition, their power was rediscovered when, after an absence of thousands of years, the demon corelings returned to plague the surface of the world.

By themselves, wards have no power. Demons, however, are infused with core magic, and wards siphon a portion of that magic away, repurposing the energy. The most common wards are defensive in nature, but a handful of wards that can achieve other effects are known, and in theory, it is possible to create a ward for any desired effect. Recently, mankind has discovered offensive wards, which can actually harm demons, who are otherwise immune to hand weapons and can quickly recover from almost any injury.

Defensive Wards:
Defensive wards draw magic from demons to form a barrier (forbiddance) through which the demons cannot pass. Wards are strongest when used against the specific demon type to which they are assigned, and are most commonly used in conjunction with other wards in circles of protection. When a circle activates, all demon flesh is forcibly banished from its line. Some examples:

Defensive ward against: Clay Demons
First appeared: *The Great Bazaar*
Description: Clay demons are native to the hard clay flats on the outskirts of the Krasian Desert. Small, they are about the size of a medium-sized dog, made from compact, bunched muscle and thick, overlapping armour plates. They have short hard talons that allow them to climb almost any rock face, even hanging upside down. Their orange-brown armour can blend invisibly into an adobe wall or clay bed. The blunt head of a clay demon can smash through almost anything, shattering stone and denting fine steel.

Defensive ward against: Flame Demons
First appeared: *The Warded Man/The Painted Man*
Description: Flame demons have eyes, nostrils, and mouths that glow with a smoky orange light. They are the smallest demons, ranging from the size of a rabbit to that of a small boy. Like all demons, they have long, hooked claws and rows of razor-sharp teeth. Their armour consists of small, overlapping scales, sharp and hard. Flame demons can spit fire in brief bursts. Their firespit burns intensely on contact with air, and can set almost any substance alight, even metal and stone.

Defensive ward against: Mimic Demons
First appeared: *The Desert Spear*
Description: Mimics are the elite bodyguards to mind demons (coreling princes), and are believed to be the most intelligent and powerful demons, short of the princes. Their natural form is unknown, but they are able to assume the form of any living thing, including other demon breeds, clothing and equipment. These demons are somewhat lacking in creativity, and so are usually restricted to taking the forms of creatures they have themselves encountered (unless directed by a mind demon). One of their favourite tricks is to take the form of an injured human and feign distress to lower the defences of their prey.

Defensive ward against: Mind Demons
First appeared: *The Desert Spear*
Description: Also known as coreling princes, mind demons are the generals of demonkind. They are physically weak, and have little in the way of the natural defences of the other corelings, but they have vast mental and magical powers. They can read and control minds, communicate telepathically, and kill with their thoughts. By drawing wards in the air and powering them with their innate magic, they can create almost any effect. The

other corelings, great and small, follow their every mental command without hesitation, and will give their lives to protect them. Sensitive to even reflected sunlight, mind demons will only rise on the three-night period of the new moon cycle in the hours when night is darkest.

Defensive ward against: Rock Demons
First appeared: *The Warded Man/The Painted Man*
Description: The largest of the coreling breeds, rock demons can range in height from six to twenty feet tall. A hulking mass of sinew and sharp edges, their thick black carapaces are knobbed with bony protrusions, and their spiked tails can smash a horse's skull in a single blow. They stand hunched on two clawed feet, with long, gnarled arms ending in talons the size of butchering knives and multiple rows of bladelike teeth. No known physical force can harm a rock demon.

Defensive ward against: Sand Demons
First appeared: *The Warded Man/The Painted Man*
Description: Cousins to rock demons, sand demons are smaller and more nimble, but still among the strongest and most armoured of the coreling breeds. They have small, sharp scales, a dirty yellow almost indistinguishable from gritty sand, and

they run on all fours instead of two legs. Rows of segmented teeth jut out on their jaws like a snout, while their nostril slits rest far back, just below their large, lidless eyes. Thick bones from their brows curve upwards and back, cutting through the scales as sharp horns. Their brows twitch continually as they displace the ever-blowing desert sand. Sand demons hunt in packs, known as storms.

Defensive ward against: Snow Demons
First appeared: *Brayan's Gold*
Description: Similar to flame demons in build, snow demons are native to frozen northern climates and high mountain elevations. Their scales are pure white, blending into the snow, and they spit a liquid so cold it instantly freezes anything it touches before evaporating. Steel struck with coldspit can become so brittle it shatters.

Defensive ward against: Swamp Demons
First appeared: Mentioned in *The Warded Man/Painted Man*
Description: Swamp demons are native to swamps and marshy areas and are an amphibious form of wood demon, at home both in the water and in the trees. Swamp demons are blotched in green and brown, blending into their surroundings, and will

often hide in mud or shallow water, to spring on prey. They spit a thick, sticky slime that rots any organic material it comes into contact with.

Defensive ward against: Water Demons
First appeared: Mentioned in *The Warded Man/The Painted Man*, seen in *The Desert Spear*
Description: Water demons vary in size and are seldom seen. They are long and scaly, with webbed hands and feet, tipped with sharp talons. Some breeds have tentacles ending in sharp bone. They can only breathe under water, though they can surface for a short time. Water demons can swim very quickly, and delight in savaging fish, though they prefer warm-blooded mammals as their prey, especially those humans bold enough to dare to sail at night.

Defensive ward against: Wind Demons
First appeared: *The Warded Man/The Painted Man*
Description: Wind demons stand about the height of a tall man at the shoulder, but with head fins that rise much higher, topping eight or nine feet. Their great long snouts are sharp-edged, like beaks, but hide rows of teeth, thick as a man's finger. Their skin is a tough, flexible armour that can turn any spearpoint

or arrowhead. That resilient substance stretches thin out from their sides and along the underside of their arm bones to form the tough membrane of their wings, which often span three times their height, jointed with wicked hooked talons that can cleanly sever a man's head when they dive. Clumsy and slow on land, wind demons have tremendous power in the sky, and can dive, attack and reverse direction before hitting the ground, taking their prey away with them.

Defensive ward against: Wood Demons.
First appeared: *The Warded Man/The Painted Man*
Description: Wood demons are native to forests. Next to rock demons, they are the largest and most powerful demons, averaging from five to ten feet tall when standing on their hind legs. They have short, powerful hindquarters and long, sinewy arms, perfect for climbing trees and leaping from branch to branch. Their claws are short, hard points, designed for gripping through the bark of trees. Wood demons' armour is barklike in colour and texture, and they have large black eyes. Wood demons cannot be harmed by normal fire, but will burn readily if brought into contact with hotter fires, such as magnesium or firespit. Wood demons will kill flame demons on sight, and often hunt in groups called copses.

Offensive (Combat) Wards:

Combat wards siphon magic from a demon, weakening its armour at the point of contact, and redirect that magic as offensive force. This force can manifest in many different ways. Some examples:

Combat ward: Bludgeoning/impact
First appeared: *The Warded Man/The Painted Man*
Description: This ward turns coreling magic into concussive force. The stronger the original blow, the more power generated. It can be placed onto any blunt weapon.

Combat ward: Cutting
First appeared: *The Warded Man/The Painted Man*
Description: This ward, when etched along the length of a blade, can enhance its sharpness, allowing the weapon to cut cleanly through even coreling armour and flesh.

Combat ward: Pressure (Arlen's palm ward)
First appeared: *The Warded Man/The Painted Man*
Description: Pressure wards exert a crushing force that builds in heat and intensity the longer they remain in contact with a demon. The Painted Man has one on each palm, and has been known to squeeze a demon's head with them until it bursts.

Other Wards:
Many recorded wards have no known use, their purpose lost to antiquity. Because testing requires bringing them into contact with a demon, volunteers to conduct the research are understandably scarce. Some examples:

Sunny Pasture

Tibbet's Brook

Shepherd

Mound of Anach Tun

Vale of Bat